DEATH IN THE SQUARE

The upper-class inhabitants of the locked-gate community called Holroyd Square in Templeton, Texas are used to their sedate, private lives — and the equally private dark secrets that each of them keeps hidden from the others. But when a vicious blackmailer rudely interrupts their existence, and is then found murdered in the Square, the police must be called. Now only Assistant Chief Wash Shipp can uncover the killer and save their tattered reputations . . .

Books by Ardath Mayhar
in the Linford Mystery Library:

CLOSELY KNIT IN SCARLATT
DEADLY MEMOIR
THE CLARRINGTON HERITAGE

ARDATH MAYHAR

DEATH IN THE SQUARE

Complete and Unabridged

LINFORD
Leicester

First published in Great Britain

First Linford Edition
published 2014

A catalogue record for this book is available from the British Library.

ISBN 978–1–4448–1941–0

Published by
F. A. Thorpe (Publishing)
Anstey, Leicestershire

Set by Words & Graphics Ltd.
Anstey, Leicestershire
Printed and bound in Great Britain by
T. J. International Ltd., Padstow, Cornwall

This book is printed on acid-free paper

ARTHUR MELLINGHAM WINCHELL
(Number One, Holroyd Square)

A fly was buzzing loudly against the window in the quiet room. Arthur Winchell opened his eyes with disgust at the idea of getting his ancient bones through another day of his ninety-four years.

He was ready to rejoin Peggy and the two children they had lost during their fifty-year marriage, but the mood didn't last long, for he still found interest in watching people and their doings.

Margaret, his surviving daughter, would be getting her brood of children off to school. He chuckled. Those who told him how lucky he was to have her taking care of him and the house, didn't live with six unrestrained youngsters.

Sometimes he thought longingly of the

years between Peggy's death and Margaret's arrival. There were worse things than loneliness. Besides, he'd had the neighbors to watch, which was enough to keep anybody busy and interested.

What a bunch they were, so different but actually so much alike. Up to things they shouldn't be. He regretted that he was too old now to take part in their peccadilloes. When he was young enough he'd been cursed with a demanding conscience.

He rose and stuffed withered feet into slippers. Pulling his robe about him, he stood at the window looking out on the morning. The sun was up east of the Park, lighting the walk in front of his house to amber-gold. As he watched, someone stepped briskly out of the trees and onto the curb.

Milton Martin, out for his morning walk, Arthur thought. He watched the man stride along, his back straight, his head held high. He moved as if he owned the earth! But Arthur thought the man was hiding some weakness he didn't want the world to see.

Martin had graduated from West Point and gone away to war in the Fifties. But he returned within a year, out of the military and unwilling to discuss anything about his experiences. He had not been wounded. Crazy? Maybe . . . but it wasn't easy to get a Section Eight. No, there was something shady about the man. Arthur would have given his eyeteeth to find out what the real story was.

After breakfast, he donned his hat, took his cane, and stepped onto the veranda. The sun was high, and it was already hot, with the last of summer lingering into early September. The shady park centering the Square was cool and inviting.

Leaning on his stick, he moved carefully down the drive, across the red-brick street and into the shade of huge old oak, magnolia, and pecan trees. His favorite bench awaited him. With his handkerchief he dusted off the few dead leaves and the bit of dust that had collected there overnight.

Lowering himself painfully, he leaned back and stretched his arthritic legs. That was better. Sometimes, when he was at rest like this, he felt almost no pain at all. Although it was early, he drifted into the light sleep that overtakes the very old. He awoke to the sound of quiet voices, but when he looked around he could see no one. Evidently the speakers were beyond the privet and crêpe myrtle hedges, seated on a bench farther along the winding path.

Arthur did not open his eyes. He had learned long ago that an old man dozing in the shade is seldom noticed. He'd learned a lot of interesting things by listening to people who forgot he was there at all.

'Really!' That was Susan Overedge. Her laughter sounded cheerful, for once. 'I never would have thought of *that*.'

Arthur waited for an answer. He knew the voices of the members of the seven families living on the Square as well as those of his own grandchildren. Who was with Garth Overedge's very young wife? She seemed nice, but he had lived too long to take anyone at face value.

'It's easy. I can communicate with people all over the world.'

That was the voice of Tom Allison's crippled son Ernest, whose mother blamed Tom's Vietnam drug use for their son's disabilities. Arthur sighed. No scandal there. Just two young people chatting while Susan's toddler Jessica played in the sandbox. He could hear the squeaks of a defective wheel as Susan joggled the stroller in which her infant son, Chester, was napping.

'I can't get out without a lot of fuss and bother,' Ernest was saying. 'And I don't know anybody who'd want to come here to see me. So I use the computer to do my traveling, and it works like a charm.'

'I've never owned one,' Susan said. 'My school was too small to have them, and Garth doesn't want one at home. He says he has too much to deal with at the office to be bothered after hours. I wish he'd get me one though — maybe I'd be more human, instead of just being a cook and diaper changer.'

Arthur sensed the tension in her voice. He thought about it. Perhaps young women nowadays might not be as content with a husband and children to care for.

Susan certainly didn't sound happy.

'You could order one, if you've got the money. I could show you how to set it up. It would be . . . something to do.'

Ernest's voice was filled with longing. Arthur, at the end of his life span, could empathize with a young man shackled to a useless body. He knew how he would have felt if he'd faced the same prospect at the age of twenty-two.

He shrugged. He preferred to look back on a life, which, in general, had been satisfying and interesting, though at times it had seemed like sheer hell.

He dozed off then and only woke when the hum of Ernest's wheelchair announced the young man's departure. Head cocked against the back of the iron and oak bench, Arthur stared up through the pattern of pecan and oak leaves.

He'd slept a good while. It was almost noon, and soon Margaret would call him to lunch. What a useless way to live! And yet, given the chance to die, Arthur knew he would cling to the last shreds of his life as tenaciously as if he were young Ernest's age, instead of pushing toward the century mark.

He straightened his back and yawned. He heard Susan calling Jessica as she pushed the stroller, its wheel squeaking shrilly, toward their home at Number Three. Young Chester was making his presence known almost as loudly.

A squirrel scolded from a pecan branch overhead, and an unripe nut rattled down to plop onto the ground at the old man's feet. He cocked an eye upward. 'Back a way,' he said, 'I'd have been after you with my .22, you little bastard. Now I guess you've got me where you want me. I can't even shy a rock at you, my shoulder's so stiff.'

He frowned as Margaret's voice called him. 'She's got me where she wants me, too. One day I'm going to run off, just like a little kid, and hide from the both of you.'

He rose stiffly and started across the street. Geoffrey Holroyd waved as he passed, heading toward his own home at the base of the Square, and Arthur nodded. Geoff wasn't the man his father was, that was certain. Jesse was a womanizer from the word go, but he managed his business competently. Geoff couldn't manage a lemonade stand for a five-year-old. Though, given his drinking habits, the lemonade might have an interesting kick.

As for the old Colonel, Geoff's great-grandfather, he'd have disowned that squirt and turned him out of the house, if he'd lived to see the mess the boy made of his life. Though few of the old man's children turned out very well, to be honest. Arthur's own deceased son-in-law had been one of the Holroyd descendants, and as far as Arthur's feelings went, being deceased was the best thing you could say about Saul Leeson.

There was a musical burble from the direction of the gate that separated the Square from Richmond Avenue. That would be Overedge, coming home for lunch. Sometimes Arthur wondered if the world had actually grown so dangerous that the sophisticated electronic locks on the gates were truly necessary. Yet there they were, and every family on the Square had a personal combination programmed into the system, with controls in their cars and their living rooms.

Arthur, as usual, had memorized the tones of every one of them, so he knew who came and went at any time of day. Lying in bed at night, he kept track of who came in later than usual — or didn't come in at all. His eyes might not be what they were, and his bones might be going fast, but by God he still had his hearing, which was a comfort.

He wondered if the Holroyds had ever realized that all the gates and locks in the world weren't a dime's worth of good, because the river ran in a big loop around the back of the Holroyd grounds.

Anybody smart enough to follow the paths that flanked the stream could access the partially overgrown and sprawling gardens of the Holroyds' Big House. From there it was no trick to scale the old stone walls enclosing the lawns and gardens of the six smaller houses facing the Park.

He chuckled as he climbed the steps to his veranda. Damn fools! There wasn't a way on earth to be secure if somebody was determined to do you in. His ancient Colt revolver lived beside his bed, and woe betide any burglar who thought he'd make easy work of such an old geezer.

He'd been in two wars, and that had taught him that you protected yourself when necessary, but your time came when it came. If it hadn't come, you could walk through a rain of shrapnel, as he had done on Normandy Beach, with your men falling all around you, and come out without so much as a bruise.

As a middle-aged officer, he had seen youngsters dying on all sides. There had been boys who might've been his own sons, if he'd had any, blown apart at his elbow. He shook those memories away. No use living the past over again, particularly the painful parts. Now he had nothing but peace and ease — too damn much of it, it seemed sometimes.

He climbed the steps carefully, using his cane to keep his balance, and moved into the cool dimness of the central hall. Those who built these Victorian houses knew how to keep people comfortable in hot weather without having to shut yourself in with air conditioning. Most of the ceilings were twelve feet high, and equipped with fans to move the air.

In fact, Arthur stayed too cool, most of the time, but Margaret complained when the thermostat was set at seventy-five. He'd taken to wearing a sweater inside the house, even in August. He thought about Geoff Holroyd with envy. He and his old-maid sister, Marilyn, never turned the dratted a/c on.

In fact, 'share the wealth' was not a slogan Marilyn had ever embraced. Arthur wondered if one day the Square would wake up to find poor old drunk Geoff standing over the battered body of his tight-fisted sister.

For that matter, Arthur thought with a grin, they might find *him* standing over his own daughter, if she kept whining for money. She had a generous annuity from Saul's death, plus Social Security for the children. What did the woman do with her money, to be always begging him for extra?

He went into the breakfast room, where they always ate their light lunch. Margaret lacked her mother's gift of laughter, her sense of humor, her wit and ready tongue, but she was a good cook. And that was her saving grace. She could make a salad that tempted even a nonagenarian's appetite. The chops melted in his mouth, and he blessed the man who invented false teeth with which to chew them.

There were compensations, he thought as he stumped up the stairs to take his after-lunch nap. Things could always be worse.

SAM LEESON

Grandpa Arthur often called him Sam Hill, as in, 'What in the Sam Hill are you doing now, boy?' Sammy Leeson seldom paid attention to his mother, and though he liked his grandpa, he didn't really think of him as a person — he'd always been there and always would be.

Sammy loved living in the Square. It was so safe that his mother allowed him to wander at will through the Park and around the grounds. He wasn't at all lonely, though his siblings were in school all day.

There were too many people to watch from hidden coverts, too many conversations to listen to, while the speakers thought themselves alone. Sammy knew things that even his grandfather didn't suspect. In fact, he knew there was somebody else, a stranger, who had been sneaking into the Square at night and now, more recently, by day.

For a week, the boy had been climbing out his window after everybody was asleep, and dropping onto the porch roof. From there he could see all the back gardens on his side of the Square, plus the lawn between the trees beside the Holroyd house. He could see over the treetops of the Park into the front yards of the houses on the other side, too.

It was only after he saw the fellow sneak past near the house that he decided to keep track of him. It did no good to tell Mama a stranger was prowling around the Square. She shushed him up without listening to a word.

Grandpa was too old to be interested, he figured. His older brothers never paid him any attention, so it was up to him. If the prowler was up to something, Samuel Grady Leeson was going to find out what it was.

Today, after lunch, Grandpa was asleep in his room, in the recliner by the window with a handkerchief over his face. Mama was in her room too, mending a basketful of socks and underwear.

Sitting at his own window, Sammy saw movement across the privet-grown wall, inside the Holroyd grounds. Whoever that was had a nerve to be creeping along the side of the house in daylight, hidden only by the cape jasmine bushes.

Sammy slid out of his window, hung by his hands, and dropped silently to the upper porch just below. Shinnying down one of the posts, over the jutting roof of the big veranda, and then down to the lawn, took a matter of seconds. He crept across the park, keeping the shape of his quarry in view. To his surprise, the intruder made his way around behind the Holroyd house and into Miz Carruthers's side yard, heading toward the back. Sammy hid in the flowerbed to see what would happen, but the old lady stuck her head out and told him to go home.

Drat! He'd wanted to see what the fellow wanted, sneaking around the Square that way. Now he'd never know.

CYNTHIA CARRUTHERS
(Number Two, Holroyd Square)

Cynthia Carruthers did not employ household help. This marked her, among her neighbors, as eccentric at best, or financially embarrassed at worst. Neither was true. The reason she did her own cooking and housework was because a housekeeper surely would learn about her clandestine profession.

Geoff Holroyd, who had been her landlord since his father died, would like nothing better, she knew, than to evict her and rent her home to someone who would pay many times the price their great-grandfathers had fixed into the lease. That same lease strictly forbade any sort of work for hire taking place on the premises.

Art was *not* work as long as you didn't get paid for it. However, Cyn's watercolor miniatures had become the rage of the art world over the past two years, and now the money was pouring in. Her tiny studio at the rear of the house was concealed behind closed draperies and lit by fluorescent lights. If Geoff learned she was breaking the terms of her lease, he would send her packing.

Packing . . . the thought of putting almost four generations of accumulated possessions into boxes and moving them someplace else made her feel faint. Besides, *this* was her home.

But the letter she had discovered in the mail basket beneath the door slot had haunted her morning and poisoned her lunch. She dreaded to think what some journalist might have dug up regarding her true identity. Nothing was safe from them.

She rose from the table and went to her desk. Maybe she had been overreacting. Surely that must be true. She took the crisp sheet out of the embossed envelope and held it to the light, squinting through her half-glasses. The postmark was not Chicago, as it had always been, but the letter was from her agent:

Dear Miss Carruthers,

Enclosed you will find my check in the amount of twelve thousand dollars. Your paintings continue to sell extremely well, this representing the sale price, less my commission, for *Lilies Under Water*. A limited-edition print has been contracted as well, and individual prints will sell for a hundred dollars each. If you will consent to sign a few of these, they will bring up to five hundred each.

Your reputation is growing incredibly quickly. *If you would consent to reveal your identity* [he had written] and to appear at an exhibition, we could command even greater prices for both originals and prints.

Indeed, *Art World Magazine* has been demanding that I give them your name and address. Their editor is becoming difficult. He finds the signature 'Cyd' frustrating, and he seems determined to learn who you really are.

For that reason, I have arranged that future mail will be posted by my confidential secretary in the suburb where she lives. You may send any communication to me to her address, which is enclosed.

But surely you could come forward and make yourself known, not only to your many admirers, but also to your respectful agent,

Vernon Cogbill

Vernon had done a remarkable job of building her career, Cynthia knew. And, at her request, he had agreed to conceal her identity. His enthusiasm and hard work had succeeded far beyond the expectations of either.

Now she was in danger of losing her home through her own success. Since returning from her European schooling, she had spent her entire life within the secure confines of the Square. To leave now would probably kill her. She had never been strong, and since turning fifty, her health had slid quietly and persistently downward.

She would be like a fragile plant, uprooted from its natural growing place. It was likely that transplanting would be fatal, she brooded. She sighed and replaced the letter in the secret drawer of Papa's desk, a convenient space to conceal her guilty secret.

She turned to the bookcase behind her and took from beneath a stack the latest copy of *Art World*. The cover made her shiver with dread.

'WHO IS CYD?'

bold capitals demanded beneath the cover art, a reproduction of her own *Painted Windows*. The cover story continued:

'This recluse, whose work is the only indication that the artist exists at all, has roused both critics and collectors to unparalleled levels of enthusiasm. Although the more *avant-garde* critics consider her work old-fashioned in its clarity of line and subtlety of color, the sensory delight it arouses has wrung from them reluctant admissions of admiration.

'Who is Cyd? Unable to learn from her agent more than the bare fact of her gender, we asked a major authority for speculations as to her artistic training and possible identity.

'Ashford Noble, dean of art critics, received us in his library, whose walls hold the fruits of years of careful purchases. Many young artists made their first major sales to this authority, and most of his acquisitions are worth many times the original purchase prices. In a prominent position is a triptych of Cyd watercolors.

''Ash,' as his intimates know him, paused before answering our question.

''It may be,' he began, 'that this is a cover name for one of our well-known artists, who is now working in a totally different style from that identified with his name. The control of line, the absolute authority of the glazes as they build to their eventual impact, tell me this is someone trained by one of the best watercolorists alive, although I cannot think who it might be.

''The pictures are quite original both in design and in rhythmic flow. Perhaps the artist trained in Europe under someone relatively unknown in this country'.'

A.W.: What do you think of some people's view of her as a frail, feminine creature? Some of the subjects and quite a lot of the handling suggest that.

A.N.: It would not surprise me if this should be the work of a man — someone like Nathaniel Fielding, whose regular work is expressed in great galloping swashes of oil. The sinewy effect of Cyd's lines suggests to me the work of a man. Women tend to be less strong and straightforward.

* * *

Cynthia slapped the magazine shut and pushed it back between the larger ones. What an idiot, though she gave him credit for suspecting her European training. Certainly nobody here had ever heard of her instructor, Valenti di Castelagni, who died before he could achieve his full potential.

And they would never recognize his ornate style and bright colors in her work. She had learned control from a master, and then she'd invented her own techniques. She certainly was no oil-splashing male artist, with pipe and beard and paint-stained dungarees!

Although she hid her studio in the rear of her house, her combined study and library was at the front. Watching neighbors from behind lace curtains was the time-honored pastime of the ladies of the Square, although not one would admit it under torture. Even Cynthia, when she was mulling over a new work, spent a lot of time gazing out over the Park or, just to her right, through the wrought iron fence that separated the Holroyd house from the brick street before it.

Now, gazing idly in that direction while she brooded, she saw a movement beyond the crêpe myrtles on the other side of the Big House. She looked at the clock. Just on one. Geoff would be inside, getting drunk in his own study. Marilyn would be taking her ladylike nap in the glider on the veranda. Who could be sneaking through their shrubbery?

She rose and leaned close to the screen, trying to make out the shape. It was gone, but when she glanced downward, she looked into the eyes of Sam Leeson, Arthur Winchell's youngest grandson, who seemed to be hiding in her flowerbed behind the spirea bushes.

He looked sheepish, but he also seemed excited. 'D'you see him, Miz Carruthers?' the boy whispered. 'I been watching him for a week now.'

'Sammy, what on earth are you doing spying on the neighbors?' she said to him, her tone sharper than she intended. *Thank heaven for my thick draperies over the studio windows!* she was thinking. *The little devil might have seen me working*.

'I keep seein' that fellow,' Sam said. 'What's he up to?'

'I don't know, and you shouldn't care. You get home to your mother now, before I call your grandpa to come and get you,' Cynthia told him.

Listening to his scuttling movements among her spirea, she waited while he obeyed, then turned away. Not until she reached the studio did she think about what he had said.

Someone moving around in the Square? How was that possible? The great wall and gates, and the electronic devices, protected the inhabitants from all intrusion. Nobody locked a door, and some left the keys in their automobiles. Any stranger roaming through the shrubbery would have to drop from the sky.

She considered. Maybe she'd better go down and lock her doors. For some reason the boy's words haunted her, now that it was too late to ask him further questions.

Why? That was the main question. Why would anyone lurk here?

The families were well-to-do, it was true, but not in the fashion of their grandfathers. Her family's inherited wealth had been depleted considerably by inflation and bad judgment on the parts of the trustees. Her earnings more than made up the difference, however, and her wants were few and simple. But not all her neighbors had such a supplement to their income. There was no ostentatious wealth around the Square, in fact. Just a comfortable lifestyle.

Even the houses themselves, once admired as the epitome of taste and elegance, were now just old-fashioned and over-large. Heating them in winter cost a fortune. The cost of a paint job that would cover the gingerbread trims, the ornate decorations, and the variety of molded shingles covering their sides would feed an ordinary family for a year. And the leases called for the tenants to maintain their homes.

Cynthia shook her head. No. No thief could expect to find money lying about here. Nobody she knew kept any considerable amount at home. Then the breath caught in her throat. Reporters sometimes sneaked about, learning secrets, digging out hidden scandals. Could the person Sammy saw be the journalist from *Art World Magazine*?

Of course not. Respectable publications like that did not send their representatives creeping about like spies for the tabloids.

She locked her doors anyway, and checked the security of the downstairs screens. Then she went down the dark hallway to her studio. Leaving the lights off, she moved silently to the end of the bay window that opened onto the rear lawn.

She felt foolish, but she slid a finger behind the heavy drapery panel and lifted it, very slightly — merely a slit to which she put her eye. Cynthia found she was holding her breath as she peeked out, into the golden fall day.

A stranger stood against the wide screen of the window, his arms wrapped about his head as if to shut out the light, in order to see *into* the room. With more control than she knew she possessed, Cynthia stood still, breathing very slowly, waiting for him to finish his fruitless spying.

'Damn!' she heard him whisper. 'I wonder . . . ' His arms came down and he pushed with both hands at the screen, as if to test its strength.

She found herself giving a prayer of thanks that she had rescreened all the windows that summer. The wire gave a sort of sigh as the intruder relaxed his pressure and stepped back.

Cynthia watched him disappear into

her privet hedge, moving toward the rear. There was something vaguely familiar about his shape and gait, but she dismissed that as a nervous fancy.

Odd. Most burglars waited for darkness. Unless, of course, he had been watching the house long enough to ascertain her habits, which tended to be dependable as sunrise.

She turned from the draped window and without illuminating the dimness of the studio, dropped into the recliner. She should call the police, yet she hesitated to break the unwritten code of the Square.

The police were not allowed in, short of murder and sudden death. The Holroyds prevailed, from river to wall, and nobody disputed their rule. And telling Geoff would be worse than useless, she knew all too well.

So what could she do? A shudder racked her frail bones and she stared into the dimness, wondering if her life was about to shatter into pieces.

SUSAN OVEREDGE
(Number Three, Holroyd Square)

Susan Overedge heard her husband's car pull away toward the gates with relief. It would have been so much easier if he ate lunch downtown, as the other businessmen did. But no, he came home instead, and woe to her if she used anything left over. It pained her thrifty soul to waste food, as Garth insisted. Cooking three elaborate meals a day, caring for the children, and keeping the Victorian monstrosity of a house spotless, as Garth also demanded, took all her time and more energy than she possessed. If not for those too-brief visits with Ernest in the Park, she would never have had the opportunity to speak with another adult from morning to night.

She should have known she was in trouble when Garth brought her to the gates of the Square and she saw the huge Gothic letters spelling out HOLROYD: THE SQUARE. It had been like a step backward into the past.

No police came here, ever, and even the postman had to have a special card to get through the gate. When there was a substitute, he left the separated bundles of mail in a big locked container set into the wall.

Each tenant was responsible for caring for the walk, the street, and the segment of the Park directly in front of his or her home, since no street-sweeper was allowed within the Holroyd domain.

Most of the people were much older than she, except for Ernest, of course, but it had been months before she caught sight of his profoundly crippled shape in the wheelchair his mother pushed into the Park. It was only on fine days that she had the chance to talk with the boy, and she found herself scheduling her children's outings to coincide with his time under the trees.

Perhaps she should get a computer, as he suggested, and try communicating with other people, not only here, but all over the world. What use was Garth's supposed income if it brought her no comfort?

Of course, getting Garth to agree was another story. He was a difficult man, expecting his wife to perform to his specifications without question — and without reward. From time to time he exercised his authority by beating her, though she never just stood there and took it passively. Fighting back, however, made him even worse. She tried to put his occasional abuses of the children out of her mind. Susan often contemplated divorce. When the children were older she might take that step. But right now, even with her teaching credentials, she didn't have the funds.

Jobs were always scarce in East Texas, and when she had mentioned the bit of money her mother left her, Garth got angry and refused to answer her.

So she had hung on for five years now, growing more and more frustrated. She had begun to feel that the next time Garth stuck his big red face into hers and criticized her housekeeping, or her appearance, she might just bite his nose off.

And that thought frightened Susan. Her anger was growing more intense, and her control could disappear at any moment. Would she hit one of the children? She devoutly hoped not. Would she skewer Garth with her apple corer? That would be minimally more acceptable.

What she wanted more than anything was to go back home to Aunt Laurie, hand over the children to that calm and smiling symbol of discipline and security, and get a job teaching in some elementary school. Marriage, she had learned the hard way, meant never having time, money, energy, privacy, or harmony in the family.

She shuddered. Garth had a fit if she dared so much as to lock the bathroom door. He seemed to feel that meant she was hiding some shameful secret from him. More and more she hated him. His intention to get her pregnant again filled her with panic, and she had secretly begun using the preventive measures her grandmother had passed down to her daughters. A spoonful of Queen Anne's lace seed every morning in a glass of water had, so far, done the job.

Garth couldn't imagine why, after her earlier easy conceptions, she wasn't already pregnant. But Susan, wisely, had concealed the seed among her array of natural vitamin supplements, all of which he disdained and ignored.

She finished loading the dishwasher and turned toward her little sewing room, where she did more reading and thinking than sewing. Before she could close the door, a call from upstairs reached her ears.

'Mommieee!'

Damn, that was Jessica, and she would wake the baby from his nap if she didn't go to her at once. Susan sighed and hurried up the steep stair toward the nursery. When she opened the door, Jessica was looking out the window. She turned when the door opened and said again, 'Mommie?' She sounded frightened.

'What is it, sweetheart? Did you have a bad dream?'

'Man out there. You see?' The child pointed out and down, and Susan leaned to peer out the tall narrow window. Below, just slipping through the hedge, a brown-shirted shape flickered and was gone. Susan's heart thumped hard.

What was a stranger doing here?

Her first impulse was to run to the phone, but she caught herself. Garth would be as furious as their landlord. He hated any intrusion into their lives, and having the police rummaging about the garden would send him into a rage for days.

Susan persuaded Jessica to lie down again, and once the child relaxed, her mother drew the filmy curtain over the window. There was no need to disturb Jessica again, even if the man was still on the grounds.

Then Susan remembered her unlocked doors, front and back. She crept from the room, then ran precipitously down the steep stair and pushed the front door shut, turning the heavy lock.

A dash down the hall brought her to the back door, where, thank God, she had hooked the screen door, and her heart slowed to a more normal rhythm.

Shaken to her core, Susan returned to her sewing room and dropped into the low rocker near a window that looked out on the small rose garden she had created in the side yard.

Usually the bright colors and bank of ferns behind the roses soothed her, but today she kept looking for furtive movements among the leaves. Finally she closed the Venetian blinds and turned on the ceiling fan.

Although it had been stifled for five years, Susan had a keen mind. Now she proceeded to consider this predicament logically. She could not call the police — and she could not tell Garth, who would accuse her of being a hysterical female with the brain of a gnat.

Upstairs in the spare bedroom, at the bottom of an antique armoire her grandfather's Colt lay in a locked walnut box, along with a box of still usable ammunition. Setting her jaw, which was much firmer than her pointed chin might indicate, Susan climbed the stair again.

She kept the spare room locked, not only because of the gun, but because it also made one less job to do when Garth made his weekly inspection, wearing white gloves with which he checked for dust.

Now she took the key from her jeans pocket and turned the stiff lock. Inside the dim room the blinds were half-closed. She opened the carved doors of the armoire and felt beneath the folded quilts at the bottom for the wooden box. Placing it on the table beside the bed, she was able to see more clearly, and her breath caught. The box had been pried open, tearing the brass hinges out of the tough walnut, bending them in the process.

Grandpa's revolver was gone. And the door of the room had been locked. What in God's name was going on here?

Susan was angry now. Whoever had taken her gun might now expect to find her helpless. Was it Garth? He knew where the key ordinarily hung, beside the pantry door, and he knew where the revolver was. The last time he had attacked her, she'd been foolish enough to threaten him. Perhaps he had taken her seriously. But why on earth should he take the weapon, unless he had sensed, in that last fight, the increasing fury she felt toward him? But Garth was as insensitive as a stump, and she discarded that notion at once.

Or had the anonymous intruder come into the house while she was busy in the kitchen? Had he, in some way she could not imagine, known the gun was there, and crept up to steal it — but how could he have locked the door behind him?

Thoughts squirreled through her mind, but at last she shook her head. She might not have a revolver, but there were other weapons. Garth had bought a heavy brass fireplace set and put the black iron poker, shovel, and tongs into the storage room when she objected to throwing away perfectly good implements.

The poker was heavy, with a double prong on the business end, and a solid knob at the top of the handle. It would make a real mess of anyone who thought he might injure her children. She took down the storage room key and went out onto the narrow rear porch to unlock the door at its end. The poker felt solid in her hand, and she didn't put it down as she relocked the door.

It would live beside her in the kitchen. She would keep it beside her bed on nights when Garth worked late. Nobody was going to intimidate her, whatever his intentions.

She realized with a sudden shock that she felt more alive than she had for years. *Was this why men fought wars?* she wondered, this rush of adrenaline that made one feel both invincible and stimulated?

And if that were true — how did they feel when they actually killed someone? Was that an even more exciting rush of emotion?

Susan shivered, the heavy poker felt cold in her small hand. Could she strike someone with it? With the intention of killing?

The answer rose reluctantly in her

mind, but she pushed it down again and went to the kitchen to begin dinner preparations. She was a decent person, she thought, and the idea that she might be able to commit murder made her terribly uncomfortable.

Yet the poker remained close at hand, and when the telephone rang in the sitting room, she took it with her. The children's safety was in her hands, she understood.

Garth regarded his offspring as little more than affirmations of his fertility. If anything threatened them, it would be up to her to take care of it — and of them.

MILTON THOMAS MARTIN
(Number Four, Holroyd Square)

His name had always seemed appropriate; a poet needed a poetic name, Milton thought. His last verse to be published in *The Lyric* had received a prize, which made him believe that at last he was about to be given his due.

He should never have gone to West Point; it was the sort of Hell from which he longed to escape. Only the thought of Papa's wrath had kept him there, to graduate far down in his class. He'd hoped to get some kind of desk job, but Korea happened — he shuddered at the memory. That had been the darkest time of his life.

The disgrace he had suffered would have been unbearable if anyone outside his immediate family had known of it. It was still dreadful even now, when he was the only one left to remember. The court-martial, a dishonorable discharge, the cold horror he still felt when he thought of his men, abandoned in the snow to die while he escaped in a half-track that was the last vehicle to leave the area.

He shuddered. That terrible winter and its terror still haunted him. The faces of men frozen fast in the snow still racked his dreams. He had escaped from Korea, but he would never escape his own guilt.

Every time he watched his neighbor Tom Allison drive away, he envied the man. Tom had been hooked on drugs and booze for years, but he'd served out his time in Vietnam without disgrace. His service in the military was respected. Indeed, Milton had heard rumors that he had been specially trained in jungle warfare.

Sophia Allison blamed her husband's drug use for their son Ernest's problems, but Martin had met some of her Louisiana cousins. Crazy as bedbugs, every one of them. No, there was more likely a genetic problem there. But Sophia would rather make poor Tom miserable.

This morning, watching Sophia push Ernest's wheelchair across the street to the Park, Milton had felt sad. The poor young fellow had more problems than anybody deserved. He'd tried to make friends with the boy, but between his own shyness and the boy's intense interest in computers, they had nothing in common.

His afternoon walk was his second outing of the day. He avoided the Park and the walk around the Square. Instead, he left the house by way of the back porch and the stone walk leading to a gazebo at the back of an overgrown rose garden.

He moved quietly into a wall of privet bushes along the wall dividing the back of his property from the river. His secret gate was concealed by a tangle of honeysuckle vines, which he carefully rearranged every time he returned from an expedition to town. Trudging along the damp path beside the stream, he refused to think of the past.

Then his eyes spotted a movement beyond the screen of shrubbery. Someone was in the Carruthers property and, as he paused, the interloper dashed toward the house and plastered himself against the big rear window.

Milton dared not move, for the dried leaves underfoot might crinkle with his weight. Breathing lightly, he watched the man try to peer into the room, though Milton knew the rear chamber was unused and was always hidden by heavy draperies.

After a moment, the man turned abruptly and moved away around the side of the house.

Should he warn his neighbor of this intruder? Milton wondered. Cynthia had been very close to his family in the past, and he didn't want her endangered. Yet would someone bent on mischief dare to go about in full daylight? It was probably someone from the Square, unrecognizable to him in the glare.

He moved away down the path toward Richmond Street. Where the river turned east, he kept on the path that became the sidewalk he always used. As he swung down the block, he realized that someone was behind him, and he turned to greet any of his usual encounters on his expeditions.

It was a stranger, wearing a brown shirt and baggy pants just like those the intruder had been wearing. Although he felt a bit of a shock, he managed to nod civilly and to say, 'Looks a bit cloudy, doesn't it?'

The fellow returned his nod as minimally as possible, and hurried past him. So near to him now, Martin felt a faint sense of familiarity. Sergeant Howard had walked like that, stiff-shouldered and short-legged, a bantam rooster strut. But Howard was long dead, along with the rest of his command. Yet this younger man reminded him more and more of the sergeant as he moved quickly away down the quiet avenue toward Elmwood Street and downtown Templeton.

Milton's goal, Carl's Gallery, was quiet this afternoon, the coffee shop along the side almost empty. He went first into the gallery where local artists displayed their work. Although there were some passable watercolorists in Templeton, too many of their paintings were of old barns, bluebonnets, and woodland streams. Although pleasant, you could buy them by the gross from any print catalog. Martin was always searching for something bold and unique.

This morning there was something new. The entire end wall was a display of drawings, stark black ink on white paper, of soldiers dying on some lost battlefield. Milton disliked the subject, but so powerful were the drawings that he moved closer to study the details.

He seemed to recognize faces. Howard was there, with young Lieutenant Griffin and Clem Satterwhite, the communications corporal. Even those bodies whose faces were turned away looked like the shapes of men he had known. It was as if some survivor had come here to show him what it was he had left behind him in that Korean snowfield.

The man on the street — could he be some relative of the sergeant? Perhaps his son? Milton shuddered as Carl came up behind him and laid a hand on his shoulder.

'Come get a cuppa coffee,' the big fellow said. 'I made some pastry this morning that would make a rabbit lick his grandpaw.'

Following blindly, Milton found himself sitting at one of the little round tables, holding a steaming cup between his suddenly chilly hands. He took a long sip, almost scalding his tongue, but the hot coffee seemed to steady him. 'You don't look so good, Milton,' Carl said, dropping into the opposite chair. 'Kinda pale this morning.'

Milton swallowed, nibbled a pastry, and managed a wan smile. 'You have a new artist, I see,' he said. 'Those battlefield sketches, very graphic. Somebody new in town?'

Carl craned his neck to look back into the small gallery. 'Yep, name of Constable. Very quiet fellow, but he seems to have what it takes. I've already had sales for his work, and it only went up yesterday afternoon.

'Your neighbor Geoff Holroyd bought one, in fact: a bomber coming back from a run, shot full of holes. It seemed to shake him up, but he bought it anyway.'

It surprised Milton that Geoff would come here, to the only outpost of the arts in Templeton. Geoff seemed more like the kind to go to one of the clubs where you could buy liquor and watch scantily-clad girls sashay between the tables.

'I didn't know Holroyd liked anything but a bottle,' he mumbled, but Carl caught the words and laughed.

'He comes in here from time to time. Says I have the best doughnuts in town. He paid no mind to the pictures until this bunch went up, though. They seemed to shake him up, somehow.'

Martin had the sudden notion that perhaps those sketches were so true to the actuality of battle they spoke personally to anyone who had ever taken part in a war. Yet how could the artist have gotten those faces so true to life?

No, he was imagining that. He had been in Korea and had seen bodies in the snow, very like those in the sketches. That was all. He wondered if Geoff had seen ghosts in that bomber picture, too, but then he recalled that Geoff had been in the infantry for his formal service. Only afterward had he qualified as a pilot and joined the Confederate Air Force team that performed at air shows. It was probably his drinking that washed him out of that, in the end.

He took another sip of coffee. His hands had warmed and steadied, once he realized that his reaction was guilt, not *real* recognition. Those bodies, eyes wide, limbs sprawled, were so universal you could see anyone you had ever known among them, he was certain.

There was no possible threat from that old war. Even if a relative of one his men knew he had been an officer, how could they ever find him? His address during his service was in Atlanta. Only after his wife's death had he returned home to Templeton, where his mother lived at that time.

He turned homeward again, keeping a cheerful expression but feeling an inward quiver. Those sketches — he would like to . . . to buy them all and burn them. Surely Carl would sell them to him, and the artist would never know his work had met such a fate.

He moved more quickly, reviewing his financial status. He could manage it — the prices on the pieces were not high. Even buying the entire lot would not be expensive. With a sigh of relief, he turned up Richmond and, instead of taking the river route, he slid his pass card into the pedestrian gate and entered the calm security of the Square. Tomorrow he would call Carl and ask the price of the entire group of sketches.

As he moved across the corner of the Park toward his home, he began to hurry. The clouds were thickening now, and he knew that before dark it would begin to rain. Old Janey, his housekeeper, never thought to close the upstairs windows, and he wanted to attend to those first. Then he would check his bank balance. Come rain or shine, he intended to make a major purchase tomorrow.

Janey didn't answer his call when he entered the front door. Probably asleep with her head on the kitchen table, dreaming of the old days in the Quarter.

Janey had no use for the modern era, and the young women of her own race who acted as if they were too good to scrub floors and cook meals for white folks. It made her feel that they scorned her and the life she had lived.

He had learned not to discuss such matters with her, else she would shoo him out of her kitchen with a broom handle. Now he crept down the dark central hallway to the stair, and moved to the furniture-stuffed rooms on the second floor. With ten rooms downstairs, he had no need for the additional six up there, but he did insist upon keeping the windows open in hot weather to keep the chambers from smelling so musty.

As he came to the upstairs hall, he thought he heard something move. Rats? Surely not! He paid a fortune each year to the exterminators, and neither mouse nor roach dared set up housekeeping here.

Maybe Janey had seen the clouds and was already up here. 'Janey?' he called. 'You gettin' the windows? Looks like rain.'

There was no reply, and whatever else

Janey might be, she was not deaf. Milton felt his heart thump. He had seen that man next door earlier today. Was it possible someone had figured out the secret way into the Square? Was there even now a prowler loose in his own house?

He knew better than to call the police. Geoff Holroyd would veto that in a hurry. He did, however, hurry back down the stairway to his study, where he took his grandfather's heavy Peacemaker Colt out of the desk drawer. He checked the cylinders, though he knew the big cartridges were still there. Every six months he cleaned and reloaded the weapon. As he returned to the hall, someone came thudding down the stair, vaulted the rail some steps above the bottom, and fled down the hall, banging the kitchen screen behind him.

My God, it was true! He had just seen a prowler in his own home. Hand shaking, he took up the phone and dialed the number that connected him with the Holroyd house. Nobody answered. Maybe that was best, he decided, as his heartbeat subsided to normal rhythms. Then if he had to kill the sergeant — he caught himself — the intruder, nobody would know he had any warning.

Here in Templeton a householder could shoot someone who broke into his home without much fear of problems later. Particularly if he lived on the Square. Whoever that was, he'd better not return to Number Four, Milton thought as he laid the revolver on the desk and rummaged in a lower drawer for the box of cartridges. From now on, this would go to his room with him at night. And he'd warn Janey to lock the screens even in the daytime.

You couldn't be too careful.

OLIVIA MAYNARD HOLT
(Number Five, Holroyd Square)

Olivia limped to the window and peered down the street. Where *was* that girl? Elma seemed to get flightier every day she lived, and at almost sixty she ought to have better sense than to traipse around town, just begging to be mugged.

She sighed, remembering when she had the use of the Lincoln and a driver, when she wanted to shop or go out to a movie or a concert. These days she was lucky to walk on her own two feet for any distance. Arthritis was the very devil; she had learned the hard way.

Money was no object. She'd tried to find a suitable chauffeur to ferry her daughter on her meanderings, but people didn't want to work for a reasonable wage any more. Her parents had never paid more than five dollars a week for a driver.

Now the Lincoln sat up on blocks in the garage, covered with a tarpaulin.

Elma might rant all she wanted about learning to drive, but no daughter of Olivia Maynard Holt would ever be seen driving, no matter what others might do. Walking was genteel, at least.

Seventy years ago, when Olivia was a girl, Madame Maynard had decreed that only fast girls drove. It had never occurred to her daughter to question her edict about that or anything else. Mama was always right, and Olivia had set Mama's decrees just above the Ten Commandments.

Drat the girl! Lunch was going to be late, and this was the day Effie left at two. She stared into the Park. Sometimes Elma paused in the shade to chat with one of the other tenants. Arthur Winchell was often sitting on one of the benches, dozing in the sun. He was only some ten years her elder, but Olivia hoped she would never grow as that old man had become. He hardly knew he was alive.

As she thought of him, she saw movement among the trees. He stumped across one of the grassy patches, leaning on his cane, and she knew he was headed toward his house and lunch. Rapping her knuckles impatiently on the windowsill, Olivia didn't hear Effie's approach until the maid spoke.

'Miz Holt, I called home and little Ted's got a fever. Ma says I better come right now and take him to the doctor. We don't want him to get down with somethin' serious. That *noomonia* he had last winter done left him pretty weak.' Effie's creamy brown face was filled with worry.

Olivia sighed. 'You go on, Effie. Elma can clear away when she comes. If Ted is sick tomorrow, you be sure to call and let me know, all right? I hate to expect somebody and not have them show up.'

She didn't really like it, of course. Servants, in the old days, were properly grateful for a chance to work ten hours a day for five dollars a week. Now they had the attitude that if you didn't hire them, somebody else would.

At least Effie'd had time to fix lunch, if only Elma would get herself home to eat it! Before she left the window, Olivia turned her sharp gaze up the street to survey the Holroyd house.

Geoff Holroyd was just going in at the gate, pushing aside the drooping sprays of late roses. That bastard — she had no problem with the term — even though it applied more honestly to her own daughter.

Geoff would have cheerfully married Elma, back when the two of them were young, just to get his hands on the Maynard money. Even if he'd known she was his half-sister it probably wouldn't have fazed him a bit, though no one else knew of her long-ago liaison with Geoff's father, also a sot and a wastrel. She'd made sure *that* secret was one that nobody had ever suspected.

She snorted. He'd have been just as broke as he was now, even if he'd had her money to spend. Money didn't last with Geoffrey Holroyd. Lucky his sister was tight with a dollar. They'd both be out on the street otherwise.

Olivia looked back toward the gate that let off the Square onto Richmond

Avenue. Motorists must use the electronic code, which could be heard all the way across the Square, but pedestrians had smaller devices to insert into the slot cut into the wall itself. She now saw Elma strolling leisurely up the other side of the park, trailing behind her the wheeled carrier into which she put her library books and her occasional purchases.

It was undignified to call out the window, of course. Olivia tapped sharply on the upper pane, but it was too far. Elma didn't hear — or didn't admit that she heard. She really was becoming difficult . . .

At last Elma looked up, her feather-cut hair gleaming like goose down in the September sunlight. From that distance, she looked much younger. Hardly forty, if that, which was somehow obscene in a woman her age. It wasn't time for her mother to give up guarding her virtue, even yet. Olivia sighed.

Flighty. She'd always been that, wanting to marry Geoff, wanting to be a writer, of all impractical things, wanting to travel to Asia . . . alone!

Olivia still searched her daughter's room every time she got the chance. She no longer quite dared to destroy the notebooks of poetry and short stories she found there, but she knew by their presence that Elma would never grow into a sensible, dependable person.

She found herself hoping that arthritis or even a minor heart problem might slow down her daughter. Only then could Olivia give up this strict surveillance and her tight control of the Maynard money.

Her late husband had helped her set up a trust for their combined fortunes, and that was all that had kept Elma from taking off on her own before now. Only marriage would have freed her, and by now that was out of the question.

As Elma strolled toward home, Olivia suddenly found herself wondering exactly what it was that her daughter did on her days out. Every Tuesday, Thursday, and Saturday she left home at nine in the morning and didn't return until noon. It seemed almost as if she were going to some job. A worse thought occurred to her. People . . . surely people did not have assignations so early in the day! Did they? She shook away the idea and turned toward the breakfast room, where lunch was waiting.

Yet even when she was settling into her chair, across the table from her daughter, she was still disturbed. How did one question one's child about such matters? Particularly when she was certainly no longer a child?

She managed a smile. 'Did you have a pleasant morning?' she asked. Elma handed her the jellied chicken, and she absently scooped a spoonful onto her plate. 'It seems odd that you have such a . . . regular . . . schedule for shopping.'

Elma's brown eyes opened wide. 'Do you mean that you have actually noticed what I'm doing? I am flattered. You never seemed to know I was gone at all. I've been working at the library for the past ten months, if you care to know.'

Olivia felt her heart jolt in her chest. 'Working?' she managed to squeak. She struggled for control. 'What do you mean, working? No Maynard needs to earn money!'

'I run the children's library from nine-thirty until eleven-thirty, three days a week. They pay me a hundred dollars a week for my efforts, and I have been putting it all away for my trip.'

'Trip?' Olivia hardly managed to get the word out, so tightly were her jaws clenched.

'To China. I've been saving all year for the tour. Teachers and librarians from all over the country are going, and the tour agency has given us a very good rate. Mr. Henley is looking forward to it almost as much as I am.'

'Mr. Henley?' This came out as a whisper.

'The head librarian. We've been planning this for some time. He and I and Miss Johnston from the high school are the contingent from Templeton. Two are coming from the Dallas library, and two from Tyler. There will be about fifty, with those from other states.' Elma was looking impossibly young. It was downright indecent!

With a mighty effort, Olivia pulled herself together. 'I forbid it. Henley's a widower, isn't he? The scandal! No, you cannot go even if you should earn the money for yourself. If I must lock you into your room, you will not set foot outside this house again without a chaperon.'

'Mother, you are truly a dinosaur. We are in the twenty-first century, remember? Queen Victoria has been dead for generations. I've been able to get out of that room since I was fifteen. Why do you think the magnolia branch outside my window is so slick? I've practically worn the bark off it, over the years, when I wanted to go out without your bothering me about it.'

Olivia sank back into her chair, fanning herself feebly with her napkin. She had never dreamt of such duplicity. It must be the Holroyd blood; the Maynards had always been the very souls of propriety.

Her own single lapse was so long ago, so well concealed, that she never gave it another thought. She had been married for five years when Elma was born. Oscar accepted the child as his own. No, that was so minor as to be negligible.

But she had no intention of allowing her daughter to commit a similar error. Something must be done . . .

'My heart!' she gasped.

'Your heart, my foot!' Elma snorted. 'Don't give me the maternal guilt act. You tried that when you broke up Geoff and me. I knew it was just a way to separate us, so now I keep in close touch with Dr. Jennings. He says you're as healthy as a horse.'

Olivia made a silent resolve to change doctors, though she feared it was too late for that to be of any good. She must find something else to keep her wayward daughter at home.

Elma dabbed her lips and put down her napkin. 'I'll get the dishes into the washer before I go. I promised to go back this afternoon and fill in for Lucy. She has the flu.'

When Elma was gone, Olivia tottered into her bedroom on the second floor and stared at her mother's portrait — what would Mama have thought?

She laid her head back on the hard cushion that had tortured her for much of her eighty-three years. 'Mama, where did I go wrong?' she asked in her most pitiful tone.

Mama knew her too well for comfort. The hard brown eyes were like marbles, staring her down as they always had. 'I'm weak, I know,' she sobbed. Surely in the privacy of her own bedroom she might be forgiven so un-Maynard-like a weakness as tears.

'Perhaps if I should die . . . ' she said aloud to Mama, but those eyes gave her the lie. Elma would dance on her grave and then go on about her wild plans with all the money in the world to help her along.

'Damn!' said Olivia Maynard Holt.

This time she thought she caught a hint of sympathy in Mama's oil-painted gaze. For the first time in her life, she wondered if Mama had suspected Elma's parentage. She'd been awfully old, of course — and then Olivia gasped. Mama had been years younger than Olivia was right now. Of course she knew!

Nobody had ever fooled her about anything.

Now, under those stony eyes, Olivia began to blush scarlet, from her toes upward.

ELMA HOLT
(Number Five, Holroyd Square)

As she loaded the dishwasher, Elma grew calmer. Confrontations with her mother always sent her blood pressure to astronomical levels. Doctor Jennings had warned her that if things continued like this, Olivia might well outlive her.

She'd often asked herself why she hadn't left when she was still young and ambitious. Money wasn't all that important, she knew, but it had seemed vital to have enough to live on. Between the Trust and her mother, she'd had no control over the funds that were nominally her own. Worse, she had never been allowed to learn anything for practical purposes like earning a living.

If she'd married Geoff — she laughed aloud. Mama had done her a great favor back then. Geoff the drunkard wasn't somebody she would want to be shackled to, and she had thanked her mother silently for saving her from a miserable mistake, although admitting it would have given the old woman too strong a hold over her.

Now, after living for decades in her mother's shadow, Elma had finally learned what was important and what wasn't. Money was necessary in amounts that would keep you alive and healthy. Her hundred dollars a week at the library did that, if she were thrifty. She had gauged the cost of her food, what her rent for a single room in one of the old homes in Templeton would be, and prices of her small necessities. She could survive on her paycheck, if she had to.

James Henley, the head librarian, assured her that she could, and in the past two years she had come to respect his opinions. Indeed — she smiled as she thought of him — she had warmer feelings for him than that. Although she would never tell her mother, the two of them planned the China trip to be their honeymoon.

It might seem silly she mused, for a fifty-nine-year-old woman to think of honeymoons. Yet after a lifetime of solitude she had finally found an intelligent companion who also stirred her heart.

James consented to keep their marriage a secret, and she had returned home last Saturday at noon, just as if they had not made that quick trip to the minister's house and said their vows. In her purse, right now, was a certified copy of her marriage certificate.

'It's going to be hard enough to handle Mama over the trip,' Elma had told her new husband. 'To hit her with a son-in-law at the same time is just more than I can manage. Let's wait until we get back. Then I'll move out, and when she comes around to accepting the inevitable, she can visit us at your house.'

His long face had wrinkled into a boyish grin, and he'd given in gracefully. She understood all too well what a gem of a husband she'd found. If it required telling Mama off, Elma would do it without regret. Olivia had never showed mercy to anyone; why should she expect it from the one she had wronged the most?

Elma looked up at the big clock that kept the household rigidly on schedule. It was almost one o'clock. She switched on the dishwasher. Grabbing her purse she called, 'I'm going now, Mama. Be back about four-thirty!' She slammed the door behind her. Years ago, Mama would have made her come back and close it like a lady. She giggled aloud.

'I am getting flighty in my old age,' she told herself. Somehow, that didn't bother her a bit.

She saw a small shape skitter across the park and into the Winchell house. Sammy, of course. What had he been doing? He ran as if he were frightened.

She shrugged off the thought. Sammy was in hot water most of the time. Whatever he'd been doing, poor Margaret had enough on her hands without bothering her with more. Thank God she and James were too old to worry about having children!

As she inserted her card in the

pedestrian gate, Garth Overedge's Lincoln slid silently to a halt and his electronic opener burbled. She smiled in greeting, though she didn't really care for the man. She had found him to be far too interested in her and her mother's affairs. He was the sort who could smell money a mile away. Helping elderly widows out of their savings would be just about his style.

He nodded back, his gaze assessing the cost of her dress. She knew what he was thinking: 'Here is a wealthy woman, living with her even wealthier old mother. How can I manage to make a profit from them?'

The Lincoln glowed in the sunlight, its deep garnet finish the shade of one of the old roses that bloomed beside the Holt gate. The double gates swung open, and the vehicle ghosted forward silently onto Richmond.

As Elma moved through the smaller opening, she said aloud, 'We've got a Lincoln too, Mr. Overedge! And when I get back from my honeymoon, I'm going to learn to drive it, even if Mama has ten heart attacks.'

She blushed. Sophia Allison, across the Square at the house opposite the Holt dwelling, had been standing beside her gate, training up a rose vine of her own. Had she heard? And if she did, what would she think?

Elma ran down Richmond Avenue, turned right on Elmwood, and fled up the library steps. 'James!' she called, seeing the big room empty. 'James, I almost let the cat out of the bag. Will you take me in, if Mama throws me out in the street?'

He came out of his office, burly, bearded and cheerful. He looked like a huggable teddy bear, and she proceeded to demonstrate the truth of her theory with enthusiasm.

'That's what I'd like best,' he said, when they disentangled themselves. 'Then you'd move into my house, and we'd be through with this ridiculous charade.'

He looked at her intently. 'Now what did she say?' he asked his wife.

'Oh, just the usual. Tried the palpitations routine on me again, but I keep abreast of that with the doctor. No, it's just that Mama never lived any life worth having, and she's bent on preventing me from having one either.

'Now I'm practically on my last legs and I have a chance to be a human being, and I'm afraid she'll do something to spoil it. My last chance to live and do things and be happy, James!' She leaned against him, taking comfort from his tweedy warmth.

'You settle down now,' he told her, giving her a gentle shake. 'We're going to have thirty years together, just like Maggie and I did. I can feel that woman sometimes when I'm just about to drift off to sleep, as if she's been staying close, trying to comfort me. And now she's letting go. I think she's really pleased I've found somebody to take care of me. She always worried about that.'

'Do you really want to live to be ninety?' Elma asked him, feeling a bit odd about having the approval of his deceased wife. Did he really believe what he said, or was he teasing her?

'With you, and if we can stay well, of course I do. Now come and let me show you where to shelve these new books we got in this morning.' He turned toward a book cart piled with bright volumes.

Elma went to work, purring like a satisfied cat. She was coming alive, like one of those Japanese shells containing hidden flowers, which when dropped into water opened and unfolded long-dried petals.

So what if Sophia had heard? Even if she told Mama, it made no difference. Now Elma was married, with James to help her if she needed it. What could Mama possibly do to stop her now?

What could anyone do? Suddenly she knew that if anyone even tried to put a spoke in her wheels she would react with considerable determination, if not with violence.

The old Elma was dead and buried. This new one put up with no nonsense.

ERNEST ALLISON
(Number Six, Holroyd Square)

Ernest enjoyed his brief visits with Susan Overedge. She was the only person near his age with whom he had any direct contact, although he communicated with literally thousands of people on his computer. Her children were annoying, but it was worth it to talk with an intelligent person who looked him in the eye as she spoke.

Although she never said much about it, she seemed as isolated as he was, and he thought she might get almost as much out of using a computer as he did.

Ever since Garth Overedge had moved his family into the Square, Ernest had been unfavorably disposed towards the man. His mother called the man a self-centered boor, and for once Ernest agreed with her.

He finished his lunch and went up to his room, using the stair-lift his father had installed for him. Once he was inside with the door closed and locked, Ernest felt in control. After a short rest, he moved to the computer desk and checked his email, wondering with some trepidation if one of those mysterious messages might be posted. To his relief there was nothing except trivial communications from some of his far-flung correspondents.

He recalled the last message very clearly. He knew only too well that he had neither enemies nor friends, but he admitted to himself that it seemed to be a threat.

'NEVER THINK YOU ARE SAFE,' it had said. 'I CAN FIND YOU WHEN I LIKE.'

He couldn't imagine what that meant. He knew no one outside his family, his doctors, and the neighbors. His correspondents via the internet had never seemed quarrelsome or hostile, though he had seen several exchanges between others on the Net that got pretty hot. He merely observed what went on in the cyberworld, feeling that it made him somehow a part of the stream of real life.

Had someone been reading his hesitant and infrequent postings and found some threat or hostility there? It seemed impossible, for he had commented only upon unemotional matters. Ernest was terrified of feelings, and the thought of revealing his own was totally repugnant. Surely he couldn't have made an enemy on the net!

He shook away the thought as he sank into the world of electronic communications. Only at such times did he forget his useless body, for here he was as strong, as quick and effective, as anyone could possibly be.

SOPHIA ALLISON
(Number Six, Holroyd Square)

Sophia stood outside her son's door, listening to the quiet clicking of computer keys. Until he found that outlet, her son had belonged to her, body and soul. Although she would never have admitted it, she had reveled in the handicap that bound him to her forever. Tom was now so isolated and withdrawn that their son provided her only reason for existence. She could spend only so much of her time in the gardens, pruning and fertilizing her flowers into intricate patterns, and watching others in the Square who led *real* lives.

Today she had seen Elma Holt hurry to the gate, her face as happy as if she were twenty instead of nearly sixty. She looked as if she had suddenly made a life for herself, after existing so long under her mother's thumb.

Sophia cringed. She'd had the chance for happiness with Tom. She had accepted him before he went overseas, and when he returned there had been no question in her mind about marrying him.

She could not believe Tom was addicted to drugs. If she refused to listen, it didn't exist. How wrong she had been! She accepted part of the blame for Ernest's handicap. She had blindly married his damaged father.

She turned from the door and moved soundlessly down the stairs. The worst thing was that there was nothing for her to do. She kept the house spotless with frenzied spasms of energy, cooked more than they could eat, and yet her empty days were taken up with long periods of sitting and waiting.

If only she had some talent or interest to busy her hands and mind, she might be more content. But instead, the hours stretched before her, barren and dark.

She sat in the parlor with the blinds drawn against the glare of the August sun and stared at the wall.

I am going mad, she thought. She sat there until her internal clock told her it was time to finish making dinner before Tom returned from work. As she rose, cramped after sitting so long, she heard a furtive step on the porch beyond the blinds.

Was someone there?

A neighbor would have called out to her. It could not be Ernest. Tom would have entered by the side door if he had come in early.

She breathed deeply, trying to clear her head. The front door stood open as always in hot weather, for no one bothered to lock their doors in the Square.

Ernest! She must protect him. Armed with a mother's courage — and a brass statuette from a side table, she peered cautiously down the hall toward the front door.

A shadow and the sound of a quiet step in the hall made her cringe and gasp silently. She raised the statuette for attack and steadied herself to face whatever danger this might be.

She did not pause to reconnoiter but charged into the hallway, around the Victorian coat rack, and straight at the shadowy figure who had almost reached the foot of the curving stairway.

'Get out of my house!' she shrieked, bringing the heavy figurine down onto his shoulder. 'Go away! Or I'll . . . I'll smash you!'

Then the statuette was gone out of her hands and she was flying backward under a tremendous blow that flung her against the wall, stunning her. With a rush of feet and a swirl of air, the stranger was gone, leaving behind no trace of his passing except the brass figure on the floor and Sophia sprawled near the stair.

Panting for breath, Sophia struggled up and staggered to the front door, which she locked securely. The side door seemed very far away, but she made it there and locked it before moving to the last, the one onto the rear porch. Then she dropped into a chair in the big, dim entry hall and let her heart settle down and her breath slow again to its normal rhythm.

She knew what should be done, but she shared the distaste of all her neighbors for any intrusion into their sanctuary. Police did not come into the Square. However, now she was forewarned. Her son was in danger, and if anyone came into her house again who might do him harm, she would be ready.

Sophia went into the study and took Tom's .38 automatic out of the desk drawer. With trembling fingers, she snapped the action to make sure it was working smoothly before loading it. Then she moved into the kitchen, donned an apron with large pockets, and dropped the gun into the one on the right.

A glance at the clock told her it was past time to begin baking the casserole, but she turned the oven to high and sat beside it, watching so as to avoid burning the food. Fresh snapped beans went into the microwave at their proper time, and potatoes simmered in creamy sauce.

By the time she heard Tom's car, Sophia had herself well in hand. A crisp salad was on the table in the dining room.

She ignored the faint quiver in her stomach.

She would not tell Tom, she decided. She would not call the police, although she could quietly warn Geoff Holroyd that an intruder had found a way into the Square. During dinner she was uncommonly pleasant to Tom. Despite her resentment and his problems, he had always been kind to her and their son. He worked hard and, if need be, he was big and strong and knew how to fight. He'd learned other things than doing drugs in Vietnam.

He smiled at her and, with a sudden rush of warmth, she returned the smile.

'You're in a good mood tonight,' he said, as he helped her clear the table. 'You look — I don't know — younger somehow. I haven't seen you like this in a long time.'

'Maybe I have a reason,' she teased. How long had it been since they teased each other so lightheartedly?

Strangely, she *did* feel better than she had in years and, as she moved up the stairs with her husband, she realized what the reason was. She had a purpose again, for the first time in how long? She was the protector of the house while Tom was gone, and if she had to kill the intruder it would not bother her much.

For the first time in months, she and Tom made love with more than habitual pleasure. Indeed, she felt again the passion she had known when they first married.

She rose the next morning, her mind at rest and her heart steady.

If *he* came back today . . .

She watched Tom's departing car, listening for the tune that opened the gate. If the intruder came back today he would find himself in very deep trouble.

She got Ernest settled in the Park, calling out to Susan Overedge, 'Will you see that Ernest gets in if it rains? I have to see Mr. Holroyd for a minute, and the sky looks threatening.'

It was the first time she had ever asked such a favor, but the young woman seemed to like Ernest well enough. God knew, there could be no hanky-panky between them, and it was good for him to have friends.

Heading toward the Big House, she realized that she had never considered Ernest's feelings before. She had thought only of what she wanted and needed. It was strange how her whole outlook had changed she thought, as she pushed open the gate to the front garden.

Marilyn Holroyd was on the porch, watering her ferns. 'Why, Sophia, what brings you here so early?' she asked.

'I need to talk to Mr. Holroyd,' Sophia replied. 'Something . . . odd . . . happened yesterday. I think he ought to know about it.'

Marilyn looked startled, but she nodded toward the open front door. 'Just step in and call. He's in the study, I think.'

Sophia smiled and followed her directions. Sure enough, Holroyd sat in his big chair, his face already flushed with the morning's libations.

'Mrs. Allison, what may I do for you?' he asked.

'Mr. Holroyd, there was a prowler inside my house yesterday afternoon at about four o'clock. I was in the parlor when I heard someone on the porch. By the time I went into the hallway, a man was about to climb the stair. I hit him with a statuette, and he knocked me down. I did not call the police, but I am now armed. I thought I should inform you of this.'

He stared at her, eyes wide and mouth open. 'You attacked a stranger who had barged into your house? Mrs. Allison, that was very brave . . . and very foolish of you. But thank you for informing me. I shall be alert for any further intrusion.

'But how on earth could anyone get into the compound?' he went on. 'It's so unlikely.' He frowned. 'No, you keep your doors locked. I'll warn the others to do the same. I do hate to call in the Law. It just isn't our way.'

'I know. Nor mine. Thank you.' She turned and left the house, nodding to Marilyn, who was watering the plant baskets that hung from a heavy steel rod.

Geoff Holroyd won't do anything but get drunker, Sophia thought savagely. But

I will be on guard. I will save us all, if I have to shoot someone in order to do it.

Instead of feeling guilty about her thought, the idea intoxicated her.

ARTHUR MELLINGHAM WINCHELL

Arthur hated stormy afternoons. The damp got into his bones, and the slash of rain against his window reminded him of the rains he had endured during wartime. He could hear cannon fire embedded in the thunder, and that was something he had heard too much of, in his two wars.

Still, he sat at the window and watched the whipping branches, the spray of rain off the porch roof, and the misty outlines of the other houses. After a time young Sam entered his room.

'Ho, Sam Hill,' he said, as the boy settled beside him onto a footstool. 'Bored?'

'Grampa . . . ' The child's voice sounded almost frightened. 'Grampa, have you seen any strangers around here?'

Arthur's hand rested on the boy's head. He kept his voice calm as he said, 'I thought I did earlier this week, but my eyes aren't what they used to be. I might have been seeing things.'

'Well, I saw somebody sneakin' 'round the Square. He went along 'side the Colonel's, down between the houses. He was over at Miz Carruthers's place, down the block at the Allison's, over behind Mr. Martin's . . . all over the place, at first at night, but the last couple of days in daylight too.'

'Boy, how do you know all this? You been sneakin' out at night? Your mother would have a fit! With a stranger around it could be dangerous.' Arthur's heart thudded faster than usual, and he thought with relief of the loaded pistol in the drawer beside his bed.

Sam shook his head. 'I go out the upstairs window onto the porch roof. From there I can see all up and down, if it's a clear night with a moon. I told Mama, but she never hears a word I say, even when I told her that man kind of looks like Daddy.'

Arthur sat up straight. 'You sure?' he asked.

That would be an interesting situation, he thought, as he waited for Sam's reply. His son-in-law, Saul Leeson, supposedly had died in a traffic accident — in Thailand — where they'd cremated him and sent home his ashes. It might have been a scam, but why convince a woman with six children that she was a widow?

Sam spoke again and Arthur bent to listen. 'I haven't seen Daddy in a long time,' the boy said, 'but it sure looked like him. You know the way he used to kind of strut?'

Arthur knew too well. That cocky walk of Saul's had been typical of his attitude toward the world. 'Sam, do you know what your Daddy did for the Manford Company? Or what the Manford Company made or sold, for that matter?'

His grandson shook his head. Of course. A five-year-old wouldn't know about such things. But Arthur determined to ask Margaret. Saul had served a couple of tours of duty in Vietnam, and it wasn't impossible that he'd made connections there that would be useful to some kind of illicit import business . . . or something of the sort.

Margaret had never shown much interest in anything that made money. He wondered what she did with the rather large sums she had controlled since her husband's death. She didn't dress particularly well, and she certainly had few living expenses.

He shivered as a vicious swirl of rain lashed the glass, and he felt Sammy shiver too. There was something here that had spooked them both. He would rather be hallucinating than to have some intruder stalking those who lived in the Square.

MARGARET WINCHELL LEESON

Margaret knew Sammy was sharp — the brightest of her children and the most like her father. If he thought the stranger looked like his father, he was probably right — particularly since Saul had been blackmailing her for the past two years.

Standing at the kitchen counter, she thought hard. Her marriage had been a disaster, though at the time she thought it necessary. Her first child, Josh, had been a 'seven-month baby,' and she knew Saul had got her pregnant on purpose, partly to get his hands on her father's money and also to secure his connection to his own kin in the Holroyd compound.

Saul was in the Army, stationed in California at the time, and that fact had saved her from much of the gossip of the Square. Everyone had seemed impressed when Arthur Winchell's plain daughter hooked Geoff Holroyd's Leeson cousin, and Margaret had believed, for about two weeks, that she had gotten lucky.

But by the end of the month she understood that she was trapped in Hell with a demanding, lustful sex-addict for a husband — and no way out. She was pregnant, with no marketable skills, and too proud to ask her parents for help.

Then Saul was shipped off to Vietnam and she was relieved of her 'wifely' duties. She was bitterly disappointed when he came back on R&R, and got her pregnant again, before Josh was six months old. She was even more disappointed when he served out his hitch without getting killed.

The Manford Company's job offer with their overseas outlets had been a godsend. Although Saul made her pregnant four more times, she no longer had to put up with him more than a few times a year.

Margaret sighed. The blessed relief she had felt when the telegram arrived, with its stilted condolences and its brief description of her husband's death in the field, was something she would never have admitted to, even under torture.

The annuity, the company insurance, and the Social Security stipends for the kids, were now hers to manage and enjoy. She returned to her father's house as a respectable widow, expecting to live quietly, but content and well enough. Then, suddenly, she found her life shattered again.

* * *

It was a quiet moonless night, and she had been sound asleep. Some noise had almost roused her, she remembered, but she fell asleep again, only to wake to find a man on top of her, hairy, hot and heavy, pulling off the bedclothes and scrabbling at her nightgown. For a dreadful few minutes she believed she was being attacked by a stranger. The fury left over from the abuses of her marriage brought her up in a twist, bursting out from beneath him and grabbing the bedside clock. Without thinking, she bashed it into the shadowy head looming above her.

When she turned on the light to call the police, she first turned her victim over and saw Saul's familiar face, slack and unconscious. Her husband. Her *dead* husband. She still shuddered to recall it.

If she called the police, she would be Saul's wife again, subject to his furies and his lust. The money would be withdrawn, perhaps would even have to be repaid. Her father would not live under the same roof with Saul Leeson, she knew, for he had never liked her husband. Again she would be cast adrift, without the ability to feed her children if she left her marriage.

She brought water from her bathroom and dashed it into Saul's face, bringing him to amid snorts and groans. Once revived, he sat up and stared at her.

'Woman, what in God's name is wrong with you? I'm your husband, and I've got rights . . . '

'You're dead, and as far as I'm concerned you can stay that way. You've been gone for years on end, without a word or a sign. Your company thinks you're dead . . . '

But then he began to laugh. 'They got

me out from under just in time. I'd been doing business for them, dealing in things that they didn't want to come to the attention of customs or the narcotics people.

'Our foes ambushed me. The only way to get them off our backs was to have me die conveniently, and leave a dead end. I've finally worked my way back home, and this is the welcome I get!'

'It's all you're going to get,' Margaret muttered. 'Saul, I won't be your wife again, no matter what. Even if I have to kill you myself. How can I kill a dead man anyway? I won't have you worry my father or the children. They're good kids, even if they are yours.

'You go about your business and leave me to mine.'

He chuckled. 'You're not much to look at. Never were. No loss there. But you're drawing money on my account, and I know it. The Company made me a deal, but I've spent all the money they gave me. They'd really kill me if I showed up wanting more.

'So you're going to be my bank, Maggie, my dear, whenever I need money.' He touched his head and grimaced with pain. 'If you don't give me what I want, I'll come back to life again with amnesia. Sick and helpless.

'You won't have the money, and you won't have your precious father, and you will have me to contend with. If you pay me what I ask, however, I'll keep my distance, 'cept when I need to make a 'withdrawal,' and I'll leave you to your own devices.

'I know pretty well how much you're taking in. I won't bother the Social Security unless I need to. You can ask your old man for extra, when you need it. Now steal me one of his fresh shirts, give me all the cash you have on hand, and I'll leave.'

He grinned savagely. 'But I will be back, I will, oh I will be back.'

Since that night she had saved money desperately, stashing away every cent she could wangle from her father, along with the other income, against the return of Saul Leeson. He had come back three times so far, taking all she had each time.

And if Sam was correct, he was about to return again.

SAUL LEESON

Saul had hoped to come home from the Far East with money to burn. And he would have, if Maggie had managed his funds, but his prude of a wife never would have condoned his illicit gains from Manford.

And she seemed to stumble across everything he ever wanted to hide from her. It wasn't brains; it was pure dumb luck, he decided, every time she nosed out a bimbo he was keeping on the side or a gambling loss he'd tried to cover up with the money he stole.

Even when he was serving his first hitch in 'Nam, she had somehow known or suspected that he was involved in drugs. She kept asking him about it every time he got back on R&R, and even during his second hitch in Thailand, where he'd made the contacts that later proved so useful. When he left the military, it was a relief to get away from her and their noisy kids and go to work for the Manford Company. Too bad his own drug use led to the Thai officials' discovery of his drug and jewel contact and the primary export route.

He'd never paid the officials off because he'd put the bribe money into his own pocket. That had been a mistake, of course, though he felt a sense of outrage that this 'tiny' error had resulted in so much difficulty.

He'd convinced his superiors that one of the native contacts had squealed. They'd killed the poor sonofabitch, of course, but it had also been necessary for them to pull Saul out in a way that wouldn't compromise the others in their network.

Which was why he had to 'die'.

The idea had come to him as he strolled along an alley in Bangkok, relishing its stinks, now that he was leaving, and watching other strollers. The man in the blue-flowered shirt reminded him of somebody from the first, and he followed him as he nosed into tiny shops or bartered with sidewalk vendors. Something about the shape, the walk — and then it hit him.

This fellow was a dead ringer for Saul! Saul sauntered up beside the man and made the fellow's acquaintance.

Saul shook with him and nodded. 'Peter Edwards. I've lived here long enough to know my way around. If you want the really good stuff,' he indicated the tray of merchandise in front of them, 'I can take you to some dealers I've done business with.'

'I'm Steve Sharrod.' The tourist beamed. 'That's mighty nice of you. I thought those trinkets looked kind of tacky, but what do I know?'

'Well you just follow me. My car is at the hotel. I'll take you to one of the legitimate dealers. You won't mind if I make a quick stop, will you?'

He left Sharrod at a bar while he got his car, making sure nobody saw him. The man came out to get in with him and he pulled cautiously out into the narrow way. When he offered his passenger a drink,

Sharrod didn't hesitate. In five minutes he was fast asleep.

Once in the outskirts of the city, Saul took a narrow track leading into the boonies, where he stopped at the end of a cart trail and heaved Sharrod into the driver's seat. With three terrible blows, Saul demolished the face that was unlike his own, although the hair was a close enough match.

He whistled softly. Two men came out of the brush and stared at him inquiringly. Saul nodded. They could arrange a car accident that would deceive anyone, he knew. He'd used them before, for other such tasks. Before nightfall, Steve Sharrod was burned beyond recognition — and Saul Leeson was dead.

He left Bangkok in a riverboat headed for Singapore. There a representative of the company provided him with a fake passport, plane tickets, and cash. In two days he was back in L. A. The money in his pocket had not lasted long.

* * *

Saul whistled as he strolled along the path flanking the river and the Holroyd garden wall. He had returned several times for financial transfusions from Margaret. Each time she was more resistant, forcing him to become more resourceful to pry the cash out of her.

One day she would dig in her heels, he knew, and he would have to find another source of income. With her father in the house, he didn't quite dare to pull any rough stuff. He well remembered the revolver the old man kept at hand.

But there were others here to be fleeced. His cousin had no money, and his tightwad sister was a hard case, but the tenants were all well off. He'd managed to find a few peccadilloes some of them might pay well to conceal.

With the access along the river trail, he was able to do plenty of peeking and peering over garden walls, listening through windows, and taking inventory of the possible prospects

He had begun following those who went away each day, ostensibly to work.

Garth Overedge, for instance, was spending two afternoons a week with a woman two blocks off Richmond. Saul knew Garth had knocked his family around a bit as well, and that should be worth something, with the child abuse laws these days. Silence was golden, they said.

And Cynthia Carruthers was evidently doing something odd in her back study. The draperies were never open, though he had detected light behind them, even on the warm days when everyone else had their windows flung open and their ceiling fans running.

He had visited his great-uncle Jesse often as a child, and, except for the most recent arrivals, he knew all the families on the Square. Everybody had something to hide. As Saul snooped and sneaked about, he was learning each and every little secret.

That was what made him happy as he strutted along, thinking of the damning papers he had unearthed in Milton Martin's upstairs study. Now he knew something really nasty.

Milton had deserted his men during

battle in Korea. And he had been court-martialed and dishonorably discharged. Martin might not have a lot of money, but Saul figured he could dig up enough to keep *that* nasty secret hidden from his neighbors.

Behind Geoff's house, Saul crept along the thick hedge to the low wall separating the Holroyd garden from that of old man Winchell. He slid across and climbed over into the pathway behind the wall beyond, making his way to the end of the row of houses.

He didn't like Olivia Holt. As a boy, he had been a great one for hiding and listening to the grownups. He remembered something that was nagging at him. Something he'd overheard in the parlor.

It was about Olivia and her daughter, Elma. Something that made his Great-Aunt Hattie's voice go tight, as if she smelled something nasty. 'That woman,' she had said, 'has the gall to continue living here under my nose. And I am forced to be civil to her! How she can . . . ?' — and here he had heard her sniffling, even hidden as he was under the stair just outside the parlor door.

Who had been with her in the parlor? Not that it mattered. He had a pretty sound idea that Uncle Jesse had carried on the family tradition of skirt chasing, and it was more than possible that Olivia hadn't moved fast enough to escape him. Or wanted to, for that matter.

There was something about Elma Holt that reminded Saul of his cousin — and himself. The Holroyd frame *was* distinctive. Elma was beginning to interest him too. He'd known her rather well, when she was younger. Now she didn't look as old as she should, as if she had found some secret fountain of youth. A lover, perhaps?

It was his aim in life to hunt out and share in any such secrets, no matter whose they might be. He had followed Elma, keeping to the other side of the street once she left the Square yesterday.

The disappointment of finding her at the library all morning bothered him. The woman was hiding something. Olivia thought so, too — he had watched the old woman as she tapped impatiently on the windowsill. Those two would bear close investigation. There was big money there.

He had thought he had a hot lead with that handicapped Allison boy and Susan Overedge, but that proved to be a dead end. The boy was so crippled up he couldn't chase a skirt if he wanted to, and she was just being nice to him. Nothing devious going on there.

Saul had stolen several small but valuable items out of some of the homes in the Square while he plotted his next move. Milton Martin would never miss the gold chains and jeweled pendants from his mother's jewel box in her locked and cobwebby room. His Holroyd cousins had no idea of all the tarnished antique silver cradled idly in felt-lined boxes in the darkened pantry.

Mrs. Allison had surprised him on his last trip into her house, but her husband would probably not miss his father's antique dueling pistols for years. Saul felt he owed Sophia a little something for that blow she had struck, however. The bruise from her blow was still dark on his shoulder.

His best haul, however, had been the truly valuable pistol hidden in an upstairs room in the Overedge house. He had ransacked the place from top to bottom, carefully returning everything to its place and relocking both the wardrobe and the door. They probably would never think to check on the firearm.

Already he had a bid from a shady dealer for enough to keep him for a while. Even if Maggie cut him off, he would strip the Square of its inhabitants' cash and valuables before he took off for greener pastures.

But what he really hoped was to make far more from the careful use of the secrets he unearthed than from his petty pilfering.

Martin was the one to begin with, he thought. He was a sheep waiting to be fleeced. Most of the tenants of the Square were, in fact. There wasn't a one who would stand up to Saul Leeson, he was absolutely certain.

CYNTHIA CARRUTHERS

The letter earlier in the week had been shock enough. Cynthia was now staring at something worse than she could have imagined. Who would have thought that she, too shy to go out into the world on her own, would be a victim of blackmail?

It was printed in neat capitals on a blank sheet of paper, then slipped through her letter slot. As she read it, she realized how terribly it could impact her quiet life:

> Cynthia Carruthers I know what yure doing in that bak room. If you want to keep your secrit youll put five thousand dollars in twenties in a paper sak and stick it in the hedge behind your propty tonight. You dont want me to tell, now do you?

It was unsigned, but she knew it must be from the dark intruder against her back screen who had managed, somehow, to learn about her use of the study for painting. She couldn't believe he had seen through her thick, lined draperies. She was always so careful to keep them tightly closed.

Yet here, in her hand, was proof that someone had spied on her. Someone who spelled and punctuated badly — or someone wanting to give that impression.

Cynthia might be fragile, but she was not stupid. Now she sat, letter in hand, and stared at the window through which she had seen Sammy Leeson, earlier in the week. The boy had been about to tell her about something he'd seen — why hadn't she listened? Now she had a chilling conviction that he might well have told her something important, if she hadn't sent him home so quickly.

What if he told Geoffrey? She would have, according to the lease, only ninety days to find a home and move all her 'personal effects, furniture, and other appurtenances' out of this dear old house that was like a part of her own body.

The money was of no consequence to her. She had the twelve thousand dollar check from her agent in hand. Instead of depositing it, she could just as well cash it. If she called the bank and sent a messenger to arrange the matter, Mr. Hargraves, the manager, would wonder why she needed so much cash. He might refuse to hand it over unless she was there to assure him she was not being coerced. Which, of course, she was, but *he* must never know that.

She would have to venture out to the bank, deposit *this* check, but keep enough cash out for her needs. She wondered suddenly what Hargraves had thought of the large deposits to her account from an agency in Chicago. But perhaps the computer handled all that, and the bank manager never actually saw the checks . . .

If she doubled the amount the blackmailer asked for, would that hold him off longer? Her years of mystery reading assured her that he would want more. But she could keep extra cash at home from now on, just in case she received another such letter.

She shivered and took down the big family Bible, then carefully placed the letter between two pages. Father would be appalled, but she must be sure nobody accidentally found it. She would have destroyed it, but she might need it at some point. You never knew what to expect next, she had learned over the course of her lonely life.

So seldom did Cynthia venture out of the Square that she found her neighbors taking an interest in her appearance, dressed as she was for town. Margaret Leeson, vigorously sweeping the walk in front of Number One, peered through the intervening trees and waved.

Old Arthur, sitting on his usual bench in the Park, raised his cane in salute, and Susan Overedge, pushing the stroller and leading her daughter by the hand, called out a greeting. As Cynthia's heels clicked past the Martin house, Milton appeared on the porch and nodded.

He looks distraught, she thought in

sympathy, returning his nod. She suddenly had the intriguing thought that perhaps he, too, had received unwelcome mail. Perhaps she wasn't the only one in the Square with a secret.

Olivia Holt was in her garden, tending her roses. She and Cynthia had never been close, but now Olivia stared at her as if she could see right into the middle of her soul. Cynthia sped to the pedestrian gate, where she pushed her card into the slot, heard the electronic burble, and shot through onto the paved apron leading out to Richmond Street.

Her handbag weighed heavily on her thin arm. It would be even heavier coming back; she might have to take a cab. Her heart was racing irregularly, warning her to slow down, breathe deeply, and keep herself calm and centered. Before she turned off Richmond onto the cul-de-sac where the bank formed a part of a small outdoor mall, she had herself in hand. It was not every day that she had to pay off a blackmailer.

Simon Hargraves was not visible when she entered the bank, and Cynthia breathed a sigh of relief. Holding herself erect, she moved to the teller's window and presented the check, which she had endorsed before leaving home. 'I would like to cash this, please,' she said, her voice quivering slightly.

Rose Gill, the young woman behind the window, glanced down at the check. Her eyes widened, and she turned it over to note the endorsement. She looked up at Cynthia. 'You are Miss Carruthers?' she asked.

'I am indeed Cynthia Carruthers. I come to town so seldom that we have not met.' She drew a deep breath. 'If you have any question about it, please call Mr. Hargraves. He has known me for years.'

The girl blushed, but nodded. 'I meant no disrespect, but you must understand that with a sum of this size I have to be certain.' She gestured for Cynthia to move across the lobby to a suite of offices at the rear.

'Have a seat, please, while I speak with Mr. Hargraves. I'm sure all this is quite correct, but he must approve the transaction.'

Cynthia leaned back into the deep padded chair and sighed. She wasn't used to walking so far, and the impact of receiving that letter added to her unease. She felt as shaky as an old woman, which she refused to admit being.

Before she quite settled herself, the door opened again and Miss Gill reappeared, followed by Mr. Hargraves.

'Cynthia! Do come in, my dear,' he said. She'd forgotten how fruity his voice was. Father would have thought him a phony, she was certain, though there never had been a problem with his management of the bank.

'Simon,' she murmured, as he took her elbow and ushered her into his sanctum, where he deposited her in a chair so deep that her feet barely reached the floor.

'Now what may I do for you?' he asked. 'Surely you cannot want to carry so much cash about or to keep it in your home. If there is a problem of some kind, do feel free to confide in me. I have found more than once that depositors have been tempted to invest unwisely or to involve themselves in scams that demand cash.

For that reason, I must make very certain that nothing of the sort is involved here.'

That made sense. Cynthia had read about such schemers who preyed on the elderly. She managed a smile. 'I do appreciate your concern, Simon, but that is not my situation. I am most certainly not making any crazy investments.

'No, instead there is an unusual situation in my family — distant cousins of mine, in fact. I find that its resolution demands a certain amount of cash, which I certainly do not intend to carry on the street. I will be taking a cab back to the Square.'

'You're certain about this?' he asked, leaning forward and folding his hands on the blotter before him. 'I am *quite* discreet. You have no one making undue demands on you, I hope?'

To her dismay, Cynthia felt herself blushing. She managed to misdirect his interpretation of that. 'I am too old and set in my ways to be blackmailed for peccadilloes, Simon!' She managed a convincing laugh.

He laughed with her. 'I didn't intend to

imply *that*, my dear. I have known you for over thirty years, and you are one of the most unlikely candidates for blackmail I have ever encountered.'

'Be assured of that, Simon. I'm sorry I cannot give you more details, but that would betray the confidences of some of my distant family members. Suffice it to say, I have decided to help someone for whom I feel a certain responsibility. As you well know, I have much more money than I can conveniently spend. I take it that my checking balance and my Certificates of Deposit are still in a healthy condition?'

He nodded. 'I can certainly understand your position Cynthia. And yes, your accounts are in vigorous health. I would prefer for you to keep some of your assets in Money Market funds — but — well, that is your decision.' He touched a button beneath his desk.

Miss Gill reappeared. 'You may cash Miss Carruthers' check, Rose,' he said. 'Put it into a plain envelope, and call a taxi for her — and make sure she's in it safely while you watch.'

* * *

Cynthia returned home, after leaving the cab at the gates and entering through the pedestrian gate, feeling as if she had run a marathon. Not in years had she felt such stress.

And never had she lied so easily, she thought guiltily. What would Father think of her?

She tucked the thick envelope into a drawer and went into the kitchen for a cup of strong tea and a handful of oatmeal cookies. Then she sat down to face the reality of her situation.

She must wait until twilight, for none of her neighbors must see her creep like a thief through her own back garden. The brown paper bag waited where she kept those to be recycled, and she envisioned herself counting five thousand dollars into it.

Later that evening, when she opened her back door, the locusts were kazooing in the trees along the river, and the shrill piping of frogs filled the air. The sweet breath of her red four-o'clocks made it seem almost like a normal twilight.

Keeping in the shelter of her crepe myrtle-lined walk, she moved toward the hedge-lined wall that enclosed the rear of her property.

Cynthia tucked the bag into a handy nest of branches beside the locked gate leading to the path along the river.

Leaving the gate unlocked behind her, she fled back to the house and secured every opening.

Despite her dislike of air conditioning, she went to bed with all her windows closed, although she didn't sleep for a very long while. Afraid to rise and look out, she listened hard, straining to hear the sound of the gate's soft creak, the rustle of brown paper, the soft swish of privet leaves returning to their places.

She heard nothing, but when she checked the next morning, the sack was gone, and the gate had been, to her astonishment — and horror — relocked.

MILTON THOMAS MARTIN

Something was amiss in the Square. Even as troubled as he had been since seeing the paintings, Milton had become aware of something unusual rippling the normally smooth waters of the neighborhood.

Mrs. Allison, next door, had begun keeping a more watchful eye than usual on her handicapped son when he was out in the park. Ernest Allison's friend, Susan Overedge also seemed tense. Two days earlier, as he passed her on one of the winding walks among the trees; he noticed her lips had been taut, even when she smiled. She had seemed unable to keep her gaze from straying to small Jessica, and her knuckles were white on the handlebar of the stroller.

What was happening? Yesterday, Miss Carruthers, dressed in her town clothes, had walked down the Square and out into the street beyond. That had happened only three times in the years since Milton had returned home from the military. When she returned, she disappeared into her house, and he heard the unmistakable sound of locks engaging. Even her windows were now closed, and the sound of her air conditioner came faintly to his ears. He felt a dim sense of impending disaster, though he could not justify warning Geoff Holroyd.

He checked his mail, expecting little beyond the usual bills and ads. This time, however, there was a folded paper among the envelopes. Trash? Milton unfolded the paper, scanned it quickly then felt his knees wobble. He made his way back into the parlor and dropped into his grandfather's deep leather chair.

Staring at the thing in his hand, he found himself imagining what his family would have thought of such a threat. A dishonorable discharge was bad enough, but being threatened with exposure of it was not to be borne.

His father, he knew, would have sought

out the blackmailer and killed him on the spot. In his generation, he might have gotten away with it too. Judges and juries had always walked softly around the favored inhabitants of the Square.

Milton poured himself a stiff drink and sat in silence, sipping and thinking. It must be the intruder he surprised the other day. He must have been upstairs of course, where the family papers were stored in labeled and dated boxes — including that damning bit that was his last gift from the Army.

Was this Sergeant Howard? The fellow on the river path had resembled him. Or was this a relative of the sergeant, coming for revenge after so many years?

He thought again of the pictures at the gallery. Whoever had painted them had seen the contorted bodies, the stained snow, and the agonized faces. He put his head into his hands.

Five thousand dollars — that equaled most of the cash he had. The trust fund his father had left was tied up beyond his reach. If he withdrew what was left in his checking account, he would have to live sparsely — until his next quarterly stipend.

Yet the idea of how old man Winchell would look down his nose, how a sot like Geoff Holroyd would smile at him knowingly, and the notion of his other neighbors scorning and pitying him, filled him with despair. He would eat rose hips and poke salad and fish from the river before he would risk such exposure. With a doleful sigh he rose and made ready to visit the bank and withdraw most of his ready cash.

Then he remembered the family antiques that surrounded him. He had lived with the Victorian furniture, the cut glass and porcelain, and the sterling silver, for so long that they had become invisible to him, yet he knew that those things were of value. His cousin Ronald dealt in rare items, having sold off most of the valuable items from his own branch of the family.

Hand shaking, Milton dialed a number and heard Ronald's familiar nasal voice: 'Yes?' He felt a surge of hope. Maybe things could work out after all.

Once his cousin realized that Milton was ready to part with some of the treasures in the old home, he volunteered to come at once and evaluate the pieces.

'I need to raise five thousand — today if possible. There's a deal I'll miss out on if I don't make the deadline,' Milton told him. 'Could you possibly bring that much cash and buy some pieces outright? I stand to lose a lot if I don't get in on this in time.'

'You've got it.' So filled with glee was Ronald's tone, that Milton resigned himself to getting a fraction of the real worth of whatever the man bought. That side of the family had always been sharp traders. If he had to do this again, he'd sell to legitimate dealers who would give a fair price.

Then he thought of Cynthia Carruthers. She was artistic, he remembered. She'd spoken, once, about something in her own home that was too valuable to risk damaging with daily use and dusting. He dimly recalled her having her own antiques appraised for insurance a few years ago.

Maybe she could help him get some idea of what the things might be worth. Again he dialed, and her thin, clear voice answered. 'Cynthia? It's Milton. I need some information, and it occurred to me that you might know, since you had your family items appraised a few years back.

'You remember that Tiffany lamp in our parlor?' he went on. 'Do you have any idea what it might be worth? Just an estimate. I don't need something right down to the dollar.'

'I *do* remember that piece.' Her voice warmed. 'There was something in a magazine recently — hold on, Milton, and I'll look it up for you.'

He held the phone, as she rustled through the stack of magazines she kept beside her chair. After a few minutes, she was back, a bit breathless.

'This says that an auction house in New York recently sold a Tiffany lamp, in mint condition, with proper provenance, for fifteen thousand dollars. Does that help?'

'Bless you, Cyn, you're a lifesaver. It does indeed help — thank you. One day

I'll ask you over to tea in appreciation. Take care.' He hung up the phone and dashed for the stairs to dig out the receipt, signed by Tiffany himself, for his great-grandmother's lamp.

Ronald might moan and protest, but he was going to give nine thousand, at the very least, for the lamp and the receipt. That would leave his cousin a more than handsome profit. No way would the greedy bastard turn down the deal he was being offered.

* * *

By the time Ronald left, carrying his carefully packed purchases, Milton was exhausted. But in his hands he held ten thousand dollars in cash. He not only had enough to pay off the blackmailer, but some to set aside for future use as well.

As he snuck out into his back yard later in the evening, he felt better than he had expected to. Relief was as good as a dose of medicine, he decided. He put the bag holding the money into the fork of his cherry tree, as the note had instructed, and turned back toward the house, after unlocking his secret — perhaps not-so-secret — gate.

To his horror, he found himself looking into Cynthia's sunporch, where she was staring out at him as if wondering what he might be doing. He nodded, a brief, embarrassed jerk of the head, and strode into his house, fastening the door behind him. Tonight, he would, like Cynthia, turn on the air conditioner in his bedroom and keep all the windows and doors firmly locked.

SAUL LEESON

Saul sat in his rented room six blocks from the Square, ten thousand dollars richer than he had been the day before. This had been like taking candy from babies. The people in the Square lived such easy lives, without having to scrape and scratch to make it, that they had no idea how to handle an emergency.

While he had yet to find more damaging secrets in the other houses, he'd helped himself to some of the goods, including a nice old pistol from the Overedge house, and some antique silver from the Holroyds' locked china closet, choice bits that would bring in tidy sums from the reliable fences he knew. He would have taken stuff from the Martin house, too, if the bastard hadn't come home earlier than expected. *That* place was a treasure trove, but Martin was keeping close watch, now, so Saul didn't dare take the time to pick his way in there again.

He had watched a stranger, evidently a dealer in antiques, taking away some boxes. Martin was probably even now inventorying his possessions and perhaps even having them appraised. It wouldn't do to steal stuff that could be easily identified.

He hadn't been through the Allison house yet. Mrs. Allison had all but disabled him the other day, when she'd dealt him a blow that could have been dangerous. She had that crippled son, and he'd learned the hard way that mothers defending their young were fiercer than bandits. He had walked warily around the Allison place, trying to decide on a plan for penetrating it.

He had known Tom Allison in 'nam. That was one wild and dangerous dude, and he was willing to bet his life that not much had changed since then. He'd seen Allison go off into the jungle alone then come back a few days later with ears, fingers — even testicles — of the gooks he'd killed. Who knew what the guy would do if he thought his family was at risk.

Old Lady Holt and her daughter were something else. He already had removed a lot of their silver from the felt-lined boxes stored in the butler's pantry. It would be a long time before those ladies ever entertained again. Probably never. They were so weird he couldn't imagine anyone wanting to share the company of either of them.

The Overedge house was a total loss except for the antique pistol. The furnishings consisted of modern stuff, mostly not worth stealing. And he steered clear of Arthur Winchell's domain. If anything turned up missing there, who knew what Maggie might do? She was just crazy enough to turn him in, even if it meant losing her income.

Besides, his own brood lived there. He hadn't much affection for them, mainly because he really didn't know any of them, but blood was thicker than water. And old Arthur was still a dangerous coot who kept a revolver beside his bed and knew how to use it too. At the age of ninety-odd, the old man was probably beyond any legal punishment. If he ended up filling Saul full of holes, he probably wouldn't even go to trial.

He sighed. He should try to get into the Holroyd house again. That stuff in the pantry and china closet was all very well, but he knew the old man had kept a safe upstairs. He'd seen it when he was a boy, and the thought of it had intrigued him ever since. Who knew what might be inside?

Meanwhile, he tried to pass the time productively. He decided to go to the library. That would kill two birds with one stone. While researching the values of antique firearms he could see what Elma Holt was up to.

The library, a WPA project, had been built in the Twenties and promised to stand forever. He climbed the steep steps, wondering how they got around the handicapped access laws, nowadays. Probably had a ramp around back.

He nodded politely at the woman behind the reference desk. 'Ma'am, I need to find a book on antique guns. My father has one and he's pestering me to find out what it's worth. I thought I'd see if you have such a thing.'

She smiled, pleased with his courtesy. 'I believe we have a *Guide to Antique American Firearms* on the reference shelf,' she said.

She bustled around the end of the counter and headed for a remote corner, where she pulled down a big red volume, bound in shiny paper. 'Here you are. It can't be checked out, though.' She sounded apologetic.

'That's all right. I can find what I need without any problem. Do you have a photocopier so I can make copies? He wants to sell it, if he can get a reasonable price. Pensions don't go very far, these days . . . '

She shook her head sadly. 'I know just what you mean. You take your time, and if there's anything I can do to help, just let me know.' She gave him a wistful glance as she moved back to her post.

You haven't lost it, he said to himself. *You can still twist them around your little finger*. Except for Maggie, but he chose not to think about that.

He settled into a chair and opened the catalog, illustrated with pictures of weapons, along with current prices. He listed everything he found on the revolver. As he read, comparing notations in the book with his own scribbles, he realized he had a real prize, worth almost two thousand dollars. He could get at least a thousand for it. He believed in letting the fence make a profit. That kept them happy and cooperative.

He was about to rise and go to the copier when he heard whispers coming from behind the stacks. 'James! Stop that!'

He listened hard. Someone was doing something he might find interesting. He edged around until he caught a glimpse of two figures embracing.

The woman was Elma Holt! And who the hell was that big, bearded fellow, hugging her like there was no tomorrow!

Saul took the book to the copier and ran off his copy. 'Thank you very much,' he said, as he returned the book to the reference desk. 'I found just what I needed.'

As he went down the steps, he was chuckling. 'And a bit more. Now I've got a hold on Olivia Holt. She'll pay a lot to keep the neighbors from knowing that her daughter's canoodling with some guy in the library.'

Once back in his room he carefully placed the library information in the gun box. Then he got out his pen and note paper and sat down to compose a letter:

> Yu better find out what yore girl is doing at the libry. Shes got more than books on her mind. That big fellow with the berd had his hands all over. She ort to have betr sens at her ag. Put $5000 in a sak and hid beside yore bak porch in the big red pot, if you dont want fokes to know whats goin on.

Quivering with glee, he walked quickly down Richmond to the point where the bridge crossed the river. There he found the dim footpath that gave access to the walls guarding the perimeter of the square. Once he was concealed from the street, he moved easily to the back wall of the Holt house.

The tough old ivy was easy to climb. Once beyond the wall, he crept, concealed by the hydrangea bushes, to the porch. There he waited a moment before stepping up silently to slide his note into the mail slot. He left the way he had come, feeling the satisfaction of a task well done. It might be that this would be his last trip to visit Maggie. The pickings here were so rich and the victims so gullible that he might easily leave with enough to keep him fat and sassy for some time to come.

As he climbed the ivy back over the wall, he glanced back for some reason, and found himself staring straight into the eyes of Sam, his youngest son. The shock startled him, dislodging his grip on the wall, and forcing him to fall heavily onto the path with a thud that left him breathless for way too long.

He hadn't seen the child for years. But even if it *was* Sam, surely the boy wouldn't recognize a father he had last seen when he was no more than two years old. Those eyes had seemed all-knowing, however, as if seeing a man climbing over a wall confirmed something the kid had already known to be true.

Damn! Would he have to kill his own son to keep from being discovered?

ELMA HOLT

Elma almost danced her way down the library steps that afternoon. Soon she would leave on the China trip with her new husband, and when they returned she would move into his home. She would be free of her mother — and free of the Square.

Fall was coming. She could feel it in the faint edge of coolness in the air, and she saw it in the wash of amber that already touched the grass along the riverbank.

According to the news, in two days or so the heat would break, and it would rain. Oncc that happened, it almost never rose to summer levels again. The weather would be reasonably cool as she prepared for her honeymoon trip with James.

She entered the pedestrian gate and glanced toward home. She was late again, and Mama would be livid and she'd be made to feel like a fool. Oh, thank God for James! Soon all the pain and loneliness she'd endured would be a faded picture from the past.

Elma saw her mother sitting at the window, staring unseeingly through the glass, as if turned to stone. Olivia didn't lift her hand when Elma waved. The younger woman's heart suddenly skipped a beat, and she moved quickly up the walk and through the front gate. Was Mama all right? She was, after all, in her eighties.

'Mama?' Elma called, as soon as she was inside the hallway. She sped up the stair and paused on the landing. 'Are you all right?' Olivia turned from the window as her daughter entered the room.

'You!' Olivia spat, her voice choked, her face reddening. 'I have been informed about your disgraceful behavior at the library. I have called the authorities and you will be picked up and held for seventy-two hours pending a psychiatric examination. I won't allow any argument. After seventy-two hours, if you are not found to be insane enough for commitment to the state facility, I shall have you committed to a private mental hospital — *for your own good*!'

Stunned, Elma opened her mouth to speak, but Olivia turned away. 'I will hear nothing. Go to your room and wait to be taken away.'

Without another word, Elma sped to her room, thrust open the window and, clutching her purse, climbed out and down the tree. She was already on top of the back wall when she realized that someone had been there before her. There were broken branches of ivy trailing down, where a much heavier foot than hers had stepped.

She peered down the other side of the wall and spotted a print in the dried mud on the path. The informant *could* have delivered that nasty message to Olivia by this route. But she had no time for conjecture. Before the authorities arrived, she would be safe, with James, in her new home.

She dropped off the wall and onto the path. Her aching knees were older now than they were the last time she had pulled this stunt. Then she ran under the bridge, sticking by the river until the Pine Creek outlet offered its own little pathway running towards Aldrich Avenue — where James lived.

Panting, she slowed to a normal pace and turned off onto a walk that flanked the rear yards of the houses facing Aldrich. Feeling more like a sneak thief, than a middle-aged bride, she crept through the gate into James's backyard and, with a sigh of relief, tapped on his back door.

She heard his firm steps and called to him softly. 'I need you!' Then, to her surprise, she burst into tears. The door swept open and then she was held hard against her husband, his beard tickling her neck, his anxious voice inquiring, 'My dearest, what on earth has happened?'

'Mama . . . ' She choked and gasped for a clear breath. 'Somebody told Mama about us . . . and she's called the mental health people . . . to . . . to pick me up for observation!'

He held her at arm's length and stared

with disbelief into her face. 'But that's wonderful!' he finally said with a grin. 'Just what we wanted. Not for you to be picked up, of course. But for you to have a really good excuse to leave the Square and come home with me — where you belong.

'Nobody is going to haul *my* wife off for 'observation.' Any observing that's to be done, I'm the one who's going to do it.'

Elma sniffed hard then began to giggle. 'You're absolutely right. I can't possibly go back and live with her again after this. We have the marriage certificate. We may have to prove we're married, you know.' She felt the tears drying on her cheeks, realizing at last, how ridiculous this whole episode was.

'Not only that,' James added. 'We're going to invite Hardy, my lawyer, for dinner. There's a big roast in the oven that Mrs. Lackey left for the weekend. We can get a pie out of the freezer. We're going to have our first dinner party!'

'I don't even have a toothbrush with me,' Elma muttered as they moved toward the kitchen, which *was* smelling heavenly. 'Much less . . . ' — she glanced at him from the corner of her eye, her lips curling mischievously — ' . . . a night-gown.'

James grabbed her in a bear hug and danced her around the table. 'My T-shirt will come halfway down to your ankles, if you don't mind wearing it. Not that I wouldn't rather you didn't, of course.'

Alone with her husband in his not-yet-familiar home, without any possession except her purse, Elma suddenly felt more at ease, more at home than she had ever done in all her life. She plunked onto a chair beside the door, turned to face James, and beamed. 'I feel as if I've been let out of jail,' she said.

'Speaking of which, I need to call Hardy,' he said. 'You peep at the roast. It's on the edge of being done just right.'

* * *

By the time their guest arrived, Elma was on edge again. Mama was so determined, so commanding in fact, that she could imagine the police fanning out right now, searching for her as if she were an axe murderer.

It helped to stay busy and she puttered about, setting the table with James's everyday silver and pottery. The plain cotton napkins from the sideboard were a relief after all those years of using heavy embroidered linen that had to be bleached and laundered and ironed with great care. Olivia never left such chores to Effie, their longtime housekeeper.

Not until the last bit of cherry pie was only a ruby memory on their plates did the three sitting around the table speak of what had driven Elma to her husband ahead of schedule. Hardy pushed back his chair, patted his stomach, and said, 'Now that we are properly fortified, tell me what in the world is going on with you two.'

Prodded by James, Elma haltingly explained the episode with her mother as well as she could. 'It was clear to me that some intruder had climbed over that back wall,' she said. 'He fell too, because I could see a mark in the path where he hit on his shoulder and hip. I used to track raccoons and possums and birds along that path, when I was little. And I could easily read the signs.'

'So the famous security of the Square is a myth,' Hardy speculated. 'All the electronic gates and such in the world aren't worth spit, when you can walk right around the river bank and climb over old walls with loose bricks and heavy ivy growing over them.

'Someone may have been sneaking around the entire complex for weeks, even months. Why else would anyone have made anything of the fact that you were meeting James in the library — and that you're more than just fellow employees?'

Elma thought for a moment. 'Actually, if I hadn't been so wrapped up in planning the China trip, I might have noticed something odd before. Milton Martin, you know, the man who lives on the other side of the Square, has been selling off his family's antiques. I thought it was just because he is unmarried and has no children to inherit the things.

'But now I wonder if he's paying off

someone? And Cynthia — Miss Carruthers — next door to him, got all dressed up and walked into town a few days ago. She hasn't done that in years. Mama said when she came back in a cab, she seemed very protective of her purse.' Elma thought a moment. 'Could it be blackmail?' she asked, her voice barely audible.

Hardy glanced at James, thoughtfully. 'Maybe . . . Or it might be something entirely different. Whatever the truth may be, we know that your mother was informed *by someone unknown* about your relationship with James. If we can learn whether she was asked for money in order to keep this from becoming known, then we'll have a bit of hard evidence.'

The doorbell rang shrilly. Elma's heart sped up uncomfortably. James reached to take her hand, while Hardy headed toward the front door.

She heard his deep voice: 'Yes? May I help you?'

There was a mutter as a lighter voice spoke. She couldn't make out the words, but she feared the worst. When two sets of feet came down the polished oak of the hall, she felt as if she might faint; by the exercise of pure will, she held herself upright and seemingly calm.

'There seems to be some confusion here,' Hardy said, as he ushered a very young policeman into the kitchen.

The boy looked down at the notebook in his hand. 'We've got a warrant to pick up Miss Elma Holt for psychiatric observation. Are you Miss Holt?'

Elma rose with all the dignity she could muster. 'No,' she replied steadily. 'I am Mrs. James Henley.' She nodded toward her husband. 'You may look at our marriage certificate, if you like.'

James took the folded certificate from his wallet and handed it to the bewildered young officer. The policeman read it slowly, his lips forming the words. Then he looked up again.

'This *seems* in order. I'm just not sure what to do about this . . . '

Hardy said, 'What you do is go straight back to your sergeant. Tell him I said Miss Holt is now Mrs. Henley, and she is legally married to Mr. Henley. In the meantime, the three of us are going to

Judge Ennis's house to sort this out.' He softened his tone a bit. 'It seems that Mrs. Henley's mother has just gotten a bit . . . confused. You know how old people can be sometimes.'

It was clear the boy was puzzled. But he nodded gamely. 'I'll go tell Sergeant Phipps . . . well, I'll just tell 'im — ' and he clunked back up the hall and out the front door, closing it firmly behind him.

'We'd better go right now,' said James. 'We can wash those dishes when we get back.' Elma felt her smile growing wider and wider. Never would she have thought she'd look forward with joy to washing dishes. It must be because this would take place in her own home at last, with her own husband doing the drying.

That made all the difference.

OLIVIA HOLT

Even in her worst nightmares Olivia had never experienced such mortification — and such shame. After all the years of rigid control and discipline she had failed to subdue her own daughter. She knew that *her* mother would have disowned such a rebellious child.

Just as Olivia must do, although her heart sank at the prospect. Elma was all she possessed. She had no siblings, and her cousins, on both sides of the family, were all either dead or too old to be of any use to her.

Geoffrey Holroyd and his tenants were no more than petty annoyances to her, when they weren't actually creating problems. She had never encouraged her neighbors to call, and she never, under any circumstances, called on them. Isolation was her state of choice.

Now she waited for doom to arrive in the shape of the public health officials. She felt more alone than at any time in her life. Once the door had slammed behind Elma, as the girl went to her room, she knew she had severed any connection, however slender, that had ever existed between the two of them.

But family honor must be protected — above all else. Then she had a bewildering thought. Where *was* the family that needed its honor protected? Only *she* represented that once numerous clan. For what may have been the first time, she recalled that Elma, whatever her own faults, was no part of the Holts. Perhaps the girl had inherited her true father Jesse Holroyd's randy nature. Blood will tell, after all.

What had ever possessed her, Olivia, to dally with the old goat? Now, at the end of her life, the idea of risking such a liaison, with its accompanying potential for disaster, was abhorrent to her. That young Olivia of sixty years ago had been a silly fool. Elma, at her mature age, did not have such an excuse.

The telephone rang. 'This is Sergeant Phipps from the police department,' rasped a gruff voice. 'We need access into the Square and the gates are locked.'

Olivia suddenly realized that she would have to confide her situation to the Holroyds, since she long had refused to have one of the electronic devices installed in her house — and Elma, of course, kept their personal remote in her purse.

'I shall have to call the Holroyds and have them override the locks,' she replied, trying to keep her voice steady. 'The gates will open for you in a few minutes.'

She hung up briefly then dialed the Holroyd number with shaking fingers. She recognized Marilyn's 'Yes?' with relief.

'Miss Holroyd, this is Olivia Holt. I have a . . . medical emergency, and there are people at the gate who need to get inside. Will you — will you kindly push the override for the electronics so they can enter the Square?'

Her heart was thudding so hard it shook her entire body.

'My dear Mrs. Holt! What has happened?' Marilyn sounded shocked.

'My daughter has . . . has suffered a breakdown and must be hospitalized at once. I beg you, Miss Holroyd, to allow them to come in.'

'Of course,' Marilyn said decisively. 'Let us know how she is.' Olivia heard the distinct 'beep' as Marilyn pushed the button.

She sighed as she replaced the phone and stared out the window. The gates swung back slowly, and two vehicles, an ambulance and a police car, moved silently into the Square toward her house and parked at the curb. She knew that all her neighbors, behind the lacy parlor curtains, would be gazing avidly at this unwonted activity in their quiet enclave, just as she would, if positions were reversed.

She had not expected so much paperwork. The Holt family's unquestioned word had always been enough to make things happen. Finally, in desperation, she called on an old family friend, Judge Winkler, to get the needed approval to collect Elma from her room and haul her off, which was distressing enough.

Then, when all was ready, and she had led the way to Elma's door, she found it firmly locked against her. That was the final straw. With bitter tears in her eyes, she nodded to the officer to force the lock.

But the room was empty! She couldn't believe her eyes, until she recalled what Elma had said in anger, just days before — something about climbing down that old tree outside her window.

'She has escaped! Who knows what she'll do, in her present condition?' Olivia moaned.

The officers looked skeptical, but concerned. 'Might she be . . . dangerous?' Sergeant Phipps asked.

'Given her behavior today, I cannot guarantee that she won't be,' Olivia said, dropping into a chair in the upstairs hall. 'You must find her!' She clasped her hands firmly in her lap to keep them from trembling.

Within a few moments her house was abuzz with unaccustomed activity. Cars moved in and out of the Square, and more policemen arrived. She could imagine the speculation going on in the other houses.

As she huddled in grief and despair, Olivia had a sudden inspiration. She rose and found the telephone directory.

'There! James Henley! That's the man's name,' she exclaimed in satisfaction to Sergeant Phipps, 'You should send someone there immediately. The . . . the man she is involved with lives there, and she must have taken refuge with him. Oh, do please find her quickly, before she comes to harm!'

* * *

As time slowly passed, Olivia waited impatiently for some news of her daughter. At last the sergeant summoned her.

'Mrs. Holt, your warrant is no good to us. It's made out in the wrong name.' Phipps looked uncomfortable.

'Wrong . . . name?' She wondered suddenly if someone had informed them of her long-ago affair, and now questioned Elma's paternity.

'Yes, ma'am. She's legally married to Mr. Henley and the warrant you have is in her maiden name. She's with her husband, just where you thought they would be, in his house on Aldrich. Now ma'am, their marriage certificate is properly executed and registered at the courthouse.

'Furthermore, Judge Walter Ennis confirms that he married them himself. They're at his house now, and he says he will not act on your warrant — or any other such request.' Phipps hesitated.

'Ma'am, what on earth made you think your daughter was crazy?' he asked. 'She seems perfectly normal to me.'

'Normal! She has been working, for one thing. At the library, of all places. And she has made a . . . a . . . a liaison with the head librarian. At her age! It's obscene!'

'But she's been married to him for three months, ma'am,' pursued the sergeant. 'There doesn't seem to be anything unseemly going on . . . '

For the first time Olivia comprehended what the sergeant had said earlier. 'Married? Without my approval? What else do you need, Sir, to prove that she has gone mad?'

'Ma'am, according to your own affidavit, your daughter is . . . ' He glanced down at the paper in his hand. ' . . . she is *fifty-nine years old*. She doesn't need anybody's consent to marry. As you should well know. As for her husband, well Mr. Henley is very highly respected, both in the community, and in his field. He not only runs the library, he teaches library science courses at the university too.

'And he's not one to fool around with, either. He has lots of friends — on the University Board, the City Commission — in all kinds of places.'

Olivia felt a jolt of fury and betrayal. She had lost control. Elma had gone out on her own, without telling a soul, and had made a new life for herself, something her mother had never been allowed to do. Now Olivia was trapped here in the old home with only the portrait of her own mother for company. She would go mad!

'No!' she shouted, feeling her control ebb away. 'I will *not* allow it! She is still my daughter, and I will make her behave just as I want and expect her to behave . . . no matter what. And I will *not* pay anyone blackmail to keep her secret. I'll . . . ' But Sergeant Phipps was holding her by the arms. She felt her hands scrabbling futilely, trying to scratch and rend him.

Then blurred shapes appeared and hustled her downstairs and into a car. The last Olivia Holt saw of the Square was the face of Sophia Allison, wide-mouthed in the glow of her front porch lamp, staring at the procession as it passed out of the compound. The gates swung shut behind the car with a clang that seemed to her fogged mind to be as final as the Trump of Doom.

Olivia felt a pinch in her arm, as she was strapped in the car. Had they given her a shot of some kind? Her body grew limp. She lay back and allowed herself to sink into the fog that crept nearer and nearer. Vaguely she knew that receiving that cryptic note had set all this disaster in motion — and the shot only accelerated her journey into oblivion.

Perhaps, she thought with her last groggy moment of consciousness, *it's easier this way. There would be no more need to control anything . . .*

MARILYN HOLROYD

Marilyn replaced the receiver and stared down at the button that had unlocked the gates and allowed strangers unrestrained access into the Square. Why, she wondered, had she opened the gates without consulting Geoff?

That was always their policy, but something in Olivia's quavering voice had seemed so desperate it had moved her to action. She hurried out and down the walk to her own gate, peering anxiously through the trees toward Number Six, where Olivia's family had lived since the turn of the century. She saw cars parked along the curb, and people coming and going. The gaping space where the outer gates were normally safely closed to the outside world seemed unnatural — and a bit frightening.

Unable to bear the suspense any

longer, Marilyn quickly sped past the Winchell house and Garth Overedge's place, where Garth himself stood, mouth agape, watching two men half-carrying a babbling Olivia Holt down her front steps. Marilyn stopped, puzzled. She looked over at Garth and said confusedly, 'But Olivia told me it was Elma who'd had a breakdown. Where *is* Elma? — did you see her?'

He shook his head. 'Nope. Only the police and a man who looked like a doctor. No Elma, only Olivia. What on earth is going on?'

'I intend to find out.' Marilyn stepped forward and caught the attention of the last policeman as he locked the door of Number Six behind him and started toward the remaining car.

'I beg your pardon,' she called, as he closed the front gate behind him. 'I am the co-owner here, and I need to know what is taking place. This is a secure compound, and all this disturbance has my tenants upset.'

He looked very young and concerned.

'I guess it's no secret,' he began. 'We

got a call to pick up an Elma Holt for psychiatric evaluation. Her mother, the lady we just took away, signed the complaint.

'When we found Ms. Holt, we learned she's been married for some time and had just gone home to be with her husband. Judge Ennis vouched for both of them, and we went back to explain this to the old lady. She kind of went 'nutso' on us then, attacked Sergeant Phipps and gave him a couple of deep scratches on his neck.

'Dr. Jennings gave her a shot to calm her down and they've taken her to the hospital. I dunno what's going to become of her now. She didn't seem to be able to take in the reality of things.

'So everything's under control now. You can rest easy and lock your gates again.'

Marilyn felt breathless. After a few minutes she managed to say, 'Thank you, Officer. And I will lock the gates. Do you need anything . . . anyone . . . else?'

'No, ma'am. Her daughter's the one to make all the decisions now. I'm going right now to tell her what's happened with her mother. I imagine she and her husband will talk to you about the property in a few days — once they've had a chance to decide on things.'

Marilyn began, inexplicably, to laugh wildly. For years she had pitied poor Elma, bullied by her mother, prevented from doing anything she might possibly enjoy, in thrall, always, to the iron rules of the Holts. Now the seemingly helpless woman had broken free and was married. Now it was her mother who must face confinement and depend upon Elma to make her decisions.

How ironic! Olivia had held her neighbors in such contempt. But Marilyn, who had tended her father, old Jesse Holroyd, during his final illnesses, had heard him in his delirium betraying the fact that the sanctimonious Olivia had at one time had an affair with him. Elma was his daughter and her own half-sister, if she was willing to admit such a thing.

She had never told Geoff. It was the sort of thing he might have used against Elma, and she already had more than enough to bear. Something inside Marilyn now rejoiced that Elma had gotten free. She had never managed that herself, but she didn't begrudge it to her sister.

She turned back to Garth. 'Mr. Overedge, it seems that Olivia has been . . . taken ill. She called the wrong people, I think, and got everyone all upset, but *she's* the one going to the hospital. Elma will take care of things for her, I'm sure.'

Garth looked down at her with amusement. 'I see, Miss Holroyd. A misunderstanding, eh? Just a sick old lady.'

'Mr. Overedge,' Marilyn said impatiently. 'I might as well tell you, also, that Elma is . . . Elma has married James Henley, the library director. It may well be that learning of her daughter's marriage is what set Olivia off. Now if you'll excuse me, I must secure the gates before some intruder gets into the Square.'

Marilyn moved quickly back into her home to reactivate the gate security system. Behind her, she could feel Garth

Overedge staring at her. *What an unpleasant man,* she thought, as she secured the enclave once again. *Poor Susan . . .*

Her brother came stumbling into the room. 'D'you go outside?' Geoff asked. 'Thought I heard the door shut, an' I could swear I heard the gates open . . . ' He shook his head groggily, and she sighed with disgust.

It wasn't that Geoff was drunk again. He was *still* drunk. He seemed to be getting worse, and she had discovered no way to curtail his intake — he was courting disaster.

If only he would die and get out of her hair, she could live with that, but she had a dreadful feeling he would have a stroke or something of the sort and be a bedridden invalid. Her responsibility, of course, so long as he lived. It would be just like him.

She had nursed their father, Jesse, through *his* long and nasty final illness. Marilyn felt suddenly that if she had it to do over again she'd have caught a bus out of here to its most distant possible destination. She did not intend to be caught in that trap again.

She had been lucky with Jesse, though. The pain medication had been prescribed for him, so no one was suspicious about the outcome of the autopsy. Dr. Jenning's father had tended her father for years and knew he was near death. The extra dose she had injected on that last day was a mercy, she had always told herself, not murder.

But thinking about it now, Marilyn Holroyd came to the conclusion that she dare not take that risk twice with Geoff. She had earned her first respite through years of enduring her father's vicious complaints. Geoff was entirely too healthy to go down quickly. It would take years of deterioration for him to reach the state Jesse had been in just before his demise.

'Why am I still here?' Marilyn said out loud, startling both herself and Geoff. He looked at her in sudden comprehension, his eyes glazed but still sharp. 'I won'er that myself sometimes. You've got money. Why not go 'way and do somethin' you want, for a change? Never did get to do anything you wanted, did you, ol' girl?'

Tears formed unbidden in the corners of her eyes. Geoff *did* understand — and she had not known that before. She patted his shoulder in affection.

'You know, I just might do that,' she said. 'If Elma Holt can run off and get married with little or no money of her own, why shouldn't I at least go take a trip someplace? Geoff, for once in your life, you've had a good idea!'

'Elma? What in the world're you talking about, Marilyn?' he asked in bewilderment.

She grinned at her brother even more cheerfully. 'Elma has married James Henley from the library, and Olivia has had a breakdown over it and been hauled off to the pysch ward. Their house is empty, though I believe the police locked up when they left.'

She gave him a push. 'Why don't you go tell Arthur and Margaret? They're probably wondering what's going on, and I need to sit down and catch my breath a moment.'

Geoff moved toward the door with

unusual speed. He loved to gossip more than anything, and she knew he would spread the word up and down the Square more efficiently than any telephone could do. In the meanwhile, she would sit in her deep rocker, with her feet up on the tapestry footstool — and think about where she would go on her trip.

Marilyn had decided, at last, that it was time to get out of the Square. If she found someplace she liked better, she could simply move there. This house was a burden she had always resented. Let Geoff have the place. She'd leave enough money in trust to pay the bills and the bank could oversee Geoff's affairs.

'*I may have killed Papa*,' she said aloud, '*but I've served my time for that. Now I can get away*.'

A movement just outside the window caught her eye, and she turned to see someone moving down the front porch steps and away. Who was that? Had he heard what she said? How stupid to think out loud like that . . . she rose and sped through the house to the portico at the side. A dim shape was pushing through the bushes flanking the path to the river.

Just then Lutetia, the Holroyd's cook, appeared in the door. 'What's the matter, Miz Marilyn? You most scared me to death when you went whizzin' past the kitchen door.'

Marilyn gazed into the servant's concerned eyes. That *café au lait* face was as familiar as her own, in its structure and long-boned shape.

Her father, Jesse, had been an old reprobate — and Lutetia's mother, an earlier servant in the household, would have had no say in the matter, if her employer had decided to have his way with her. Now she wondered if Lutetia was aware they might be half-sisters — or that they might have other half-siblings all over town.

It was not something they had ever discussed, and Marilyn was too reserved to open the topic now. By all rights, Lutetia should have had a portion of the Square — and the money, but Marilyn knew Geoff would do anything to prevent *that* from happening.

Perhaps if she succeeded in escaping

from Templeton and all its baggage, she ought to send Lutetia a generous check. She could say it was in appreciation for the servant's decades of faithful service.

If she got away, and if that unknown intruder on the porch had not overheard what she had been stupid enough to say aloud. And if she could find release from the self-imposed bondage that had trapped her here for so very long.

GARTH OVEREDGE

Garth had thought when he moved his new wife into the Square, that he was securing his family from outside interference. According to local tradition, the Holroyd estate had been an impenetrable bastion for those fortunate enough to reside here.

He wasn't afraid of break-ins or criminals; he was big and strong and fearless enough, he assured himself, to take care of anything like that. No. He wished, instead, to be left alone and allowed to practice what he considered to be the old virtues and values. A disobedient wife — or child, for that matter — *must* be beaten into submission and taught a lesson. And in today's insane world that could be made to seem wrong. In fact, he had often read sensational stories about decent husbands and fathers being ostracized — and sometimes even sent to prison — for doing their plain duty. Here, inside this solid old house through whose walls no sound would ever pass, he was Master of all he surveyed.

Or he had *believed* that to be true, before he found the folded sheet, taped shut and stuck in his mail, at the office last week. His secretary, when queried, thought it might have been pushed through the slot by one of his associates or a client.

He read the thing and passed it off as such. Yet his heart continued to pound, and his face felt flushed. For once he had returned home eagerly, to make sure his wife was unchanged, and his children safe. Even then, the note reverberated through his mind:

Yu may be rite, yu may not, but fokes these days thinks its rong to beat up on yore famly. I seen what you done that nite. I herd yore wife yell and try to fite bak. If yu want to keep this between us, put $5000 in a sak and hide it along the top of yore bak fense Sunday nite. Put it under the big ivy vin so it wont blo away.

He'd managed to keep his head above water during the latest fiscal crisis and was gradually building his business back up, but Garth Overedge was shy of cash. Everything he could spare from actual living expenses was plowed back into the company.

He could not borrow anything . . . not until he repaid the outstanding loans run up to prevent bankruptcy. He must think of something else.

Recalling the old handgun that had belonged to Susan's family, he decided that if he couldn't sell the thing to a Civil War collector, he could always use it to remove this idiot from his life.

He turned back into the house, knowing that Susan was waiting to serve supper. He was a stickler for meals being served on time, and never before had *he* been the one to delay that.

The children already were in their places, Jessica sitting on a thickly-cushioned chair and the baby in his high chair. Garth insisted upon feeding them at the table, rather than earlier in the kitchen. Garth knew he must impress his will upon his children now, while they were still malleable and at his mercy.

Working such long hours, even on most weekends, he took advantage of meal-times to exercise his authority. Over his wife's objections, he questioned Jessica about her wrongdoings and admonished Chester over dropped messes. If that caused Susan to have indigestion, it was simply her own misfortune.

Tonight, however, the atmosphere seemed different. Jessica was wide-eyed and silent, contrary to her usual habit of jabbering away nonsensically. Susan's thoughts were turned inward toward something . . . worrisome? Observing the crease between her eyes and the restlessness of her hands, he could sense she was profoundly disturbed about some issue that was not, for once, concerned with him.

He set his cutlery neatly parallel across his plate, wiped his mouth on the spotless napkin, and turned to Susan. 'Would you get that Civil War pistol from your great-grandfather's box? I find that I may need a weapon, and I do not intend to buy one, with money as tight as it has been.'

She looked up, startled and pale. 'You mean *you* didn't take it out of the box yourself?' she asked, her voice barely above a whisper. 'I'd hoped it was you . . .'

Garth felt his heart thud. '*What do you mean?*' he asked, carefully. 'Why did you think *I* had taken it?'

'Because it's not there. Jessica saw a prowler. It frightened me, so I looked for the pistol. The door to the room was locked. The wardrobe was locked, but the box had been broken open, and the gun was gone.'

Her eyes filled with tears. 'Someone has been in our house!' she whispered.

'Here? In the Square? Impossible! There is every kind of security imaginable.' He stood and stalked to the window, staring out into the September twilight.

'I *saw* the man Jessica saw. She cried at nap time, and I went up, and he was there in the yard, moving away. The gates were locked. I locked all the doors and windows as well, but it was evidently too late. I . . . ' Her voice choked off into a sob.

Garth now understood with fatal finality how the author of that note had come by the information he now threatened to broadcast. 'I should call the police . . . ' he began, but he bit off the words hesitantly.

If they reported the theft of the weapon, valuable though it might be, there was a good chance the prowler might retaliate by giving the law the information he had threatened to reveal. And, he knew, husbands were now being sent to prison for doing just what he had been doing to Susan all these years.

Without saying another word, he rose, left the dining room and went upstairs to the bedroom. He didn't turn on the light, but leaned against the window screen, staring out over the lawn, the hedges, and the ivy-clad wall running behind the row of houses. Beyond that — he caught his breath, understanding how the intruder had moved through the Square at will.

The river lay beyond, and there was a

path along its bank. The wall was no obstacle to a nimble person or even a good-sized child. That bastard Geoff Holroyd had told him the lease included complete safety from intrusion, but now it was plain that meant nothing. He should have checked further before committing himself to this long-term lease.

Garth Overedge sat back on the edge of the bed, feeling his heart gallop, his blood pressure rise. If he couldn't raise the money — and he couldn't shoot the fellow without a gun — what could he do to avoid arrest?

He pulled the blinds and turned on the rose-shaded lamp. Somewhere out there, it was quite possible that someone was watching his window, gloating at the hold he had over his victim. But Garth would not allow himself to accept defeat.

He would put a bag onto the wall, all right, but filled with cut-up newspaper. He would go to work as usual on Sunday, and come home on schedule. But two could walk that river path, and two could climb that wall. He would see who invaded his privacy, and if all fell out as he hoped, he would send that blackmailer downriver without benefit of a boat.

He was, after all, in a cut-throat business. That could be extended into other areas of his life. On Saturday he'd visit a local pawnshop and buy one of their private stock of weapons, under the table and without any wait to check his record.

THOMAS ALLISON

The years had flown past in a blur for Tom Allison, like some vast river, battering the unsteady craft that he had become with wave after wave of stress and horror. His time in 'nam had affected both his mind and his body, he knew all too well, without Sophia's sharp comments to drive that home.

He had acknowledged that his failings may have caused their son's disability, and that admission had filled him with such guilt that he found it hard to communicate with the boy. It had also affected his relationship with his wife adversely. They had married in a state of misty hopefulness. Sophia had been lovely, warm, exciting. But following Ernest's difficult birth, and after the extent of his flaws were known, that bliss had begun slowly to leech away.

Tonight, when he had arrived home to find Sophia flushed, her eyes bright with a glow he had not seen in years, he had wondered what happened to cause her unusual excitement. When she did not volunteer any information, only showing warmth and affection he had thought extinguished forever, he asked nothing, but gratefully accepted the gift. He did not want to ruin this new passion by asking his wife too many awkward questions. Heaven knew he had caused Sophia enough pain over the years. He would not invade her privacy now.

Tom's frequent nightmares thrust him back into the wartime jungle again, watching comrades die in any of a thousand terrible ways. Occasionally he relived one of those lone hunts he had conducted, after drugging himself into a state in which he felt both immortal and invulnerable.

They were terrible dreams, from which he waked panting and sweating, often creeping downstairs to avoid waking his wife. They left him exhausted the next day, but he was unable to explain them to her.

Sophia's amazing change of heart, followed by their lovemaking, allowed him to sleep peacefully for once. He experienced no nightmares and, curled against her back, he had sunk into a dreamless state he had believed lost to him forever.

Tom's law practice, though demanding, was not dramatically so. He took no criminal cases, preferring to handle only corporate matters, wills and family trusts, and the like. His paralegal attended to the research and dog work, and his secretary, who had been with his father, knew the business as well or better than he did.

He frequently found himself in the position of easing corporate transfers, negotiating estates, and soothing nervous clients while dealing with their legal issues. To his surprise, he was quite good at it, possibly because his own nerves had been shattered from stress. He could recognize the same symptoms in others that had troubled him for so many years.

Suddenly, he was basking in an

unaccustomed happiness. Coming home was something to be anticipated with joy instead of dread. Last night he had found it possible to talk with his son again finding to his surprise that the boy knew much more about computers and how they worked than the so-called experts he had hired to keep the firm's systems working properly.

Floating on this roseate sea, he ran aground hard on the slip of paper he uncovered among Friday morning's mail. A threat to himself he could have dealt with easily. Endurance, after all, was something he had learned in a harsh school. This, however, inflamed him with anger, as nothing had in years:

> Yu got a son. I no how to get to him. He cant hep hisself much, so hes no risk to me. I can get him any time I want. You put $5000 in a sak and stick it in the hedge by yore bak gate on Sundy nite, els yu may not be a daddy no more. I been goin thru his computer to get at him. Hes brite, but that makes no differnce.

The cowardice of it! To threaten a disabled boy was the act of one who had no decent human instincts. Tom felt his face grow hot, as it had back in the bad old days. The blood was drumming in his ears as he drove home, and when Sophia saw his face that evening she fell silent, the glow dimming from her face.

'Tom? What's wrong?' She sounded frightened, and he wondered suddenly if she, too, had seen or heard something that made her feel insecure.

He had hidden his pain for so long that it was hard to change the habit. Now he knew, if he was not to lose Sophia again, this time — perhaps — permanently, he must communicate this threat. She might be angry, accusing, devastated, but it must be done.

He tried to smile, but his face felt as if it might crack. 'Honey,' he said as softly as possible, 'Where's Ernest?'

'He's up in his room, on the computer.'

'We've got to talk.' He fumbled in his pocket for the note, which he unfolded and smoothed before offering it to her.

Sophia looked as if he might be

handing her a death warrant. She took the paper and read it through. When she looked up, he recognized her expression. He had seen it on the faces of comrades in battle.

'I almost got him yesterday,' she said. Her face regained its color, and her eyes took on a dangerous glint. 'I was resting in the parlor when I heard someone on the porch.'

Incredulous, Tom listened to her story, thinking all the while that he had lived with this woman all these years without suspecting she had such courage and determination. 'So I'm keeping the .38 in my apron pocket or next to me when I sit down. A pistol isn't very comfortable to wear, is it? I never thought about that before,' she concluded.

Tom felt a rush of affection. For too long he had shut himself away inside his own problems, oblivious to wife and son alike, he realized. Now, when both might be threatened, he knew that he loved them desperately. They were his lifeline, without which he might sink into a swamp of despair.

He reached for his wife and hugged her close. 'My God, Sophie, if he'd hurt you . . . he didn't, did he?'

'Just knocked me down. I have a bruise or two, but he has worse. I tried to break his shoulder with that statuette.' She giggled against his shoulder. 'I always hated that thing — but it may be my favorite piece of bric-a-brac now.'

'What do you want to do about this?' Tom indicated the letter.

'If he can get into the Square, he can get into the house, even if everything's locked up tight. I've always heard that locks only keep honest people out.

'If he wants to get at Ernest, we'll either have to kill him or call the police. And who knows whether they could — or would — do anything at all?' She looked up at him, and that unfamiliar gleam in her eyes filled him with emotion.

'You know, Sophie,' Tom said. 'Ernest is a grown man now. Why don't we ask him what he thinks? He's brighter than both of us put together, you know.'

She nodded. 'We'll go now,' she said. 'It's time for him to come down for supper, and we'd just as well fill him in first.' She led the way upstairs, and Tom followed a step behind, feeling as if he once again trod a treacherous path through unfamiliar jungle, unable to judge the direction from which a fatal attack might come.

Sophia tapped on the door softly. 'Ernest? Are you ready for supper, son?'

The clicking of computer keys stopped, and the whir of the wheelchair's motor purred behind the thick door. The lock clicked, and Ernest backed away as the two came into his room.

'Dad?' It had been years since Tom had come to his room. They saw each other only in the evenings when Ernest felt like coming to the dinner table.

'We've got something to discuss with you, Ernie,' Tom began. It had been years since he'd called his son by that pet name. 'I received a note this morning, and it concerns you. Here. You read it. Then we need to put all our heads together and figure out what to do about it.'

Ernest took the note, his hand

trembling, making the paper quiver between his fingers. 'This must be what this e-mail message means. Come look. I printed it out, and I think it's still in the basket . . . '

He turned his chair and moved back toward his desk where the computer rested. He dug into a stack of printouts and handed one to Tom.

NEVER THINK YOU ARE SAFE.
I CAN FIND YOU WHEN I LIKE.

Sophie pointed, her finger shaking. 'Look at that! That note you got, Tom, was faking ignorance. There's not a thing wrong with the spelling here, and it can't be possible for there to be two different people threatening us at the same time — can there?'

Tom nodded slowly. Someone was stalking them. The thought made his hair prickle on the nape of his neck, just as it had in the jungle when he felt unseen eyes staring from the tangles of vegetation. But he kept himself under control, even though all his carefully honed instincts told him to go after the perceived threat with all his bloodthirsty skills. Instead, he asked, in his mildest tone, 'Do *you* have any thoughts on the matter, Son?'

Ernest looked into his eyes. 'Get me a gun, Dad. I can't run or hide or fight, but I *can* pull a trigger.'

The words shocked Tom profoundly. He felt himself go cold, thinking of his frail son faced with killing or being killed. How would he feel, faced with such a threat and totally unable to do anything to protect himself?

'Your mother has the .38. I'll pick you up a lighter weapon, a .25 maybe. It might be hard for you to handle anything heavier. Anyone stalking you will have to come up here, and you'll be in close enough range to do some damage.'

His son nodded. Sophia put her hand on his shoulder while Tom put his arm around her. For the first time in years, their family seemed like a real circle, united in a way that had eluded them before now. They loved one another deeply, Tom understood with joy, and what threatened one threatened them all.

He did not add that he intended to go out into the yard on Sunday night, camouflaged and armed only with his combat skills, to meet this cowardly prowler in the night. He had been taught by experts. Whoever this extortionist was, he would not find among his prospective victims any who had spilled as much blood as Tom Allison had in the deadly jungles of Vietnam.

SAUL LEESON

Saul was beginning to wonder if he were being too modest in the demands he had made upon this herd of sheep waiting to be fleeced. He had known most of these people, to some extent, for many years. He understood that they were not what others might call wealthy, but he also understood their reluctance to invite the outside world into their enclave.

Demanding more money from each might push one of them over the line and cause an unwelcome intrusion of lawmen. If he managed to take away twenty or thirty thousand dollars from this caper, he would have enough to establish himself elsewhere. If he should need more later, well he could always come back for some more judicious blackmail.

The secret, he had learned in his nefarious career, was not to ask for more than the traffic would bear. If you sheared your sheep lightly, there would always be more wool. If you skinned the beast, that was the end of the profit.

Saul had hesitated before adding Tom Allison to his list of potential victims. Tom might be dangerous, he knew. Still, he'd watched the man interact with his family since returning to the Square. There did not seem to be much love lost there. Tom might care enough to shell out enough to save his son's life, but probably not enough to go stalking whoever posed the threat.

He'd also hesitated a long time before writing to his cousin Marilyn. He remembered the times from his boyhood when she'd brought him up short. He couldn't *prove* she'd killed old Jesse, but it was what he would have done, given the chance. If she had, she might just laugh it off. Or she just might go out in the dark and leave him some cash.

He counted up his earnings so far with quiet pride. The Carruthers woman had paid off as directed, as had the coward, Martin. Olivia Holt was a loss. She'd paid nothing, and then, from what he could gather, she had gone completely bonkers.

Oh well. If she ever got out of the loonie bin, he still could threaten her with the secret he'd guessed, that her daughter was old Jesse's child. That might wring some cash out of her.

Elma, though, seemed to be a lost cause. She'd evidently gone off and married the fellow she'd been cozy with, which was a pity. He was certain she would have paid dearly to keep from being held up to scandal and ridicule.

But he had ten thousand in hand, as well as the profit from selling the other stuff. By tomorrow night he might have another ten thousand. Then he'd head to Denver, where he still had connections.

The profit from selling the stolen items would make it well worth the time and effort. Now Saul was ready to make the big killing he'd been working toward all his adult life.

Once *that* was accomplished, then Maggie could go hang. He'd never set foot in the Square again. With that welcome thought, he drifted off to sleep, dreaming of tomorrow night's rich harvest.

* * *

The next day was hot, as September usually is in East Texas. From experience, Saul felt sure that before dark there would be a thunderstorm, and the news confirmed a weather front was about to move through the Panhandle. He welcomed it. There was nothing like a hard rainstorm to keep people inside and out of the way.

He left his room and wandered to Carl's Gallery for breakfast. He chuckled at the display of paintings that must have hit Milton Martin hard. His own war had been in the jungle, but he knew a lot of guys who had served in the snows of Korea. They all had horror stories to tell about lost battles and betrayal.

The poet probably thought that display was aimed right at him. Instead it had been pure good fortune that the artist had arranged this time and this place for his show. Even as he was thinking this, the door opened and Milton Martin entered the café gallery.

Probably intended to buy the whole shooting match and burn 'em all, Saul decided. He watched as Martin sat at a table facing away from the artwork, and ordered coffee and doughnuts. The man wouldn't recognize him, Saul reassured himself. Still, he finished his meal quickly and left while Martin was absorbed in conversation with Carl.

He wandered around the shopping center most of the morning, making small purchases to keep from being noticed. By one o'clock he headed back to his room to take a nap. He needed to have his wits about him for the night's harvest of paper sacks filled with cash.

* * *

Saul woke to a growl of thunder. Good. The front was on schedule, just as predicted. By the time he walked to the river, it would be time to begin.

He donned dark clothing, jammed a folding rain hat on his head, and thrust a dark blue ski mask into his pocket. He would be able to slip into those back gardens without detection, even if his victims were watching. The rain-soaked night fell well before eight o'clock, when he began heading down Richmond toward the eastern loop of the river.

Soon he had turned off Richmond onto the path flanking the backs of the houses east of the Square. He avoided the steeper path near the river bridge. It was slick in such weather and a pedestrian there might arouse suspicion. He would retrieve Overedge's sack first then return behind the Square to the Allison fence, grabbing that contribution on his way back.

The rain was still falling in buckets, and it must be even heavier upstream. Damn! The river was rising quickly and the path was under water in places, meaning he would have to slip onto the Holroyd grounds and climb the low walls between the houses west of the Square. He used the opportunity to slip Marilyn Holroyd's *billet doux* under the screen door facing the portico.

Although he was sure his dark attire

cloaked him, he still had an uncomfortable sensation he was being watched. Once past the Winchell place, though, he would be free. He slipped along the wall, half hidden by the sodden ivy, to the spot where he had instructed Garth Overedge to secure his bag of cash.

But there was nothing there! Even as he felt about, wondering if the wind had moved the heavy loop of vine and displaced the bag, something heavy crashed through the shrubbery. He froze behind the trailing ivy.

There came a roaring flash and something hit him hard in the upper arm, flattening him against the wall. A voice yelled, 'Show yourself, you bastard! I'll shoot you again!'

His arm numb, Saul sailed over the wall without thinking about it. In 'nam he'd been careful to avoid too many dangerous missions, but his buddies had talked among themselves about such gut reactions.

He scurried, crablike along the path, close under the wall. Only when he reached a point where the river was over the bank did he creep back, his arm throbbing, over the wall. He pushed through the heavy foliage of camellias, privet, and crepe myrtle between Number One and the Holroyd place. The study window was dimly lit, so he circled the huge house until found himself, at last, in the Carruthers garden. There, he knew, the bank behind was much higher, and he left through the gate to follow a safer route.

He stopped behind the Allison house. Bleeding heavily and panting with exertion, he hoped that this final step would go easier. He climbed awkwardly up and over the gate and into the garden, where trellises of roses screened him from the house.

Again he fumbled through the wet leaves, searching for the bag. Again he found nothing.

Frightened, he turned to run, but before he could reach the gate he heard a noise from the rear. Now he would have to leave through the front or be caught. Again he surprised himself with a sudden burst of speed. Wounded and winded, he still managed to speed around the trellises and over flower beds, past the house.

Just as he reached to open the front gate, he felt something behind him, close . . . too close. He rushed out and across the street into the Park, following the winding path to avoid the muddy grass. The thunder was so loud he couldn't tell if footsteps still pursued him or not.

As he dashed between benches, over shrubbery, and around tree trunks, Saul Leeson felt his Nemesis draw near. He had one moment of absolute terror as he sensed a movement that was not the wind.

Then something hard — like iron — struck the side of his neck. He slid down into a black pit that promised no pardon — and no return.

GEOFFREY HOLROYD

Geoff Holroyd sat on his porch, his feet on the ornate railing and his gaze fixed on the attractive posterior of Sophia Allison as, in all innocence, she bent over her flowerbed, weeding the periwinkles. For all her forty-odd years, she was still nicely curved and hadn't picked up a bit of weight.

He knew she was unaware of him, for he was screened not only by distance but also by the thick swaths of wisteria cloaking the shady porch. From this vantage, he had watched many such women — some of them busy about things less innocent than weeding periwinkles.

His sister Marilyn, in the glider beyond the bow window, was unable to see Sophia. She was gazing placidly at little Jessica Overedge on the other side of the

Park. The child was peeking through the latticework that kept her from the street.

'Such a sweet little thing,' Marilyn mused aloud.

Her brother snickered. Old maids, he knew, adored children. He was incredibly relieved that his sister had never married. Neither of them had any offspring to squabble over inheriting the Square. That would have driven him round the bend.

Bad enough to have to divide their assets between them! At least she paid the household bills, which allowed him some drinking money. He'd gambled away so much of his capital that it took nearly all his small pension to keep him supplied with booze.

Reflecting on this, he turned his gaze down the peaceful quadrangle formed by his own front fence to the ornamental fences that enclosed the six houses facing each other across the wooded enclave of the Square. The high wall just visible in the distance guarded his small fiefdom from the rest of Templeton, Texas.

As he watched, a car approached and he heard the musical code activating the electronic switch that operated the distant gates. A long Lincoln slid onto the quiet street and turned into the drive on the other side of the Overedge house. Garth Overedge was home from his somewhat obscure doings in the world of Big Business.

'You know, I wondered when the bust came if that was going to put the lease beyond his means,' Geoff mumbled to his sister. 'Evidently he covered his bets somehow, because I can't see a dime's worth of difference in their lifestyle, before and after.'

'Garth Overedge is one of those people who seem to prosper no matter what the market brings,' Marilyn observed. 'I'd have *loved* to see him go. The man isn't fit company for a chimpanzee.'

Geoff snorted. He missed the usual arrival of Elma Holt, who no longer came tripping through the pedestrian gate. That woman was still nice to look at! She must be nearly sixty now, he thought, though she certainly didn't look it.

He often wondered why he had found such a prim girl so fascinating in his younger years. Probably because she was the *only* girl of his age in the Square — and the only one he hadn't managed to seduce. Her mother — blast that old bitch! — had been the reason he never got into Elma's pants; she'd kept an eagle eye on them from the start. But Olivia had got her comeuppance at last, which pleased him no end.

Now another car pulled up to the street gates and entered. That would be Tom Allison, coming home to Sophia, the periwinkle lady. Lawyers were a pain, Geoff reflected, and Allison was no exception. If Geoff's father Jesse had known Tom's father would become an attorney, when he leased the house to him right after the First World War, he never would have gone through with the deal.

Back when Jesse was alive, everybody in the Square had stood in awe of him. But Geoff had none of the respect, and it rankled.

A rumble of thunder erupted off to the northwest. The sky was turning that odd shade of gray-blue that told him it was about to rain. And blow. Summer storms were a feature of East Texas, and sometimes they could be pretty bad.

Geoff rose and held out a hand to his sister. 'Let's close the windows,' he said. 'Looks as if we're going to get a shower.'

'I hope Lutetia gets back before it really begins to pour,' Marilyn grumbled, as they made their way through the house, rushing to batten down for the storm.

While Geoff checked the last of the windows, Marilyn switched on the weather channel. 'Damn!'

'What's up? Tornado?' he asked.

'Flash flood watch. That means the river will rise, whether it rains here or up the country,' she grumped.

The rain, which had been pouring straight down, began driving in gusts as the wind slashed it against the walls and windows. It was as if somebody were playing a fire hose against the house, Geoff thought as he settled into his worn leather recliner and reached out automatically for the freshly opened Scotch bottle.

The old timbers creaked and cracked, and an icy-cold chill crept through

Geoff's bones. He pulled an old afghan over his legs and up to his chest.

'Good day to get drunk,' he mumbled. 'Any day's good for that.'

As darkness fell, the river, just within his angle of vision through the blurred windowpanes, began to rise over the low banks. At last he dropped off to sleep.

He dreamed the old nightmare. He was at the controls of a B-29, his head fuzzy, his balance off. The co-pilot was screaming at him, but his hands were frozen, even though he could see the ground below, with its long cluster of condominiums, rushing up to meet him.

He woke with a jerk, feeling again the impact and the ensuing flood of darkness. Tears dribbled from his eyes. He'd killed his whole crew and sixteen people who lived in the complex.

If it hadn't been for Dr. Jennings covering up the fact that he was drunk while piloting the plane, he'd have gone to prison — and lost everything. He seldom thought about it anymore, but today, for some reason, the memory had chilled him to the bottom of his soul.

The bottle was empty. As he struggled up to get another, he became aware of a movement just outside the window. Someone was wading through the shrubbery, he thought as he peered out into the torrent.

A flash of lightning revealed the intruder, head bent in the pounding rain, moving toward the back of the house. Geoff shook his head, trying to clear it, but his vision was blurred. When he looked again there was no one there and only the shrubbery thrashed and flapped wet leaves in the wind.

Was he having delusions now? Would he soon be seeing pink elephants dancing on the ceiling, as Marilyn threatened? Nonsense! Holroyd men could hold their liquor. Even his great-grandfather had drunk his fifth every day, and he'd died sitting on the veranda with his feet propped up on the railing, a surprised expression on his face. Eighty-seven he'd been at the time.

Geoff looked again at the window, but only his blurred reflection stared back at him. Maybe he'd seen a branch whirling across the space. The wind buffeted the house mercilessly, and more and more leaves were taking flight. He poured two fingers of Scotch into his glass from a fresh bottle, noting with pleasure that his hands were steady. No, he'd seen something real, though maybe it wasn't what he first thought it to be.

He closed his eyes and laid his head back. The smell of the study was compounded of old leather, musty paper, Scotch, and that dim scent of mildew that sooner or later permeates old Southern houses.

It sometimes made Geoff shiver, thinking himself somehow transferred back through time into his childhood. In a minute, Papa would stalk through the French doors from the parlor, his hands tucked under his coat tails, his brow marked with three precise frown creases.

Geoff had never been able to keep anything secret from Papa. He'd have known that the highest rank Geoff made in the Korean War was corporal, and his colonelcy was an honorary one given him by the Confederate Air Force demonstration team.

Whether or not Dr. Jennings covered it up, Papa would know that his son, the sole male heir of the Holroyd line, while stinking drunk, had killed sixteen people and his crew. Thank God the old bastard was dead!

LUTETIA MASTERS

That river was sneaky, Lutetia thought as she stepped onto the rear veranda the next morning and stared across the diminished garden toward the muddy waters raging out of their normal banks. The terrace beside the dock was invisible, as was the dock itself except for a tall pole that held the light standard. They'd had to shut off the electricity last night or risk shorting out the whole system.

A dead animal — something furry like a fox or a raccoon — rolled into sight and out again. Logs from upstream bumped and crushed among the crepe myrtles and cape. Probably have to replant most of 'em, because they kept getting washed out.

The water was closer to the house than it had been, and for an instant Lutetia wondered if this time it was going to keep coming and mess up the Old Colonel's pride and joy. But it never had in the hundred years since Colonel Geoff's great-grandpa built this house, and why should Nacoche River break its record now?

She pulled the garbage can around the corner into the drive, set it in its slot, and ambled toward the front gate. The wind had been something fierce last night, and twigs and branches littered the drive and walk. The Park across from the house looked tousled, and she could see debris and broken branches lying like jackstraws among the trees.

She opened the gate ready for the garbage men, and strolled over into the Park. They would have to call someone to clean up — and then she came to a sudden stop. There was a lump of something across the brick path that wasn't the normal flotsam after a flood. A face stared up at her, bloodless and blue-tinged.

Lutetia backed up a step, feeling her heart falter. What had she found, here in the safe confines of the Square? Nobody could get in unless he was admitted. She moved forward again, keeping a tight grip on herself.

Once she came close, she bent and stared at the leaf-littered face, half revealed by the position of the body, the sodden clothing, and the pale, clenched hands. Bending farther, she lifted a leafy spray and saw the great bruise on the back of his neck and the dark-edged wound in his arm.

She felt bile rise in her throat, and let the branch fall back into place. The back of this poor fellow's neck had been hit with something hard. There was a ragged hole in his dark shirt sleeve, and if it hadn't been for the rain, the whole place would be awash with blood, she felt sure. As it was, a pale pink puddle surrounded the body.

She looked down again into the blank face and saw something indefinably familiar. Somehow he looked a bit like the reflection she saw in the mirror every morning, except for the color of his skin. Could he be another of Mr. Jesse's 'indiscretions'?

Her mother had been Mr. Jesse's housekeeper, and she knew her father had been Mr. Jesse himself. And she wasn't the only one, though there were some other children belonging to his sisters somewhere. One of the great-nephews used to visit, she remembered.

This poor bastard, and she used the term deliberately, was probably another mishap. The Holroyds had all been devils with the women. But how in God's name had he come to be here in the Park in the middle of the Square without anybody knowing it? Or *had* somebody known it?

Shivering now, she turned and ran back to the Big House. 'Miz Mar'lyn! Miz Mar'lyn!' she yelled as she banged through the front door. 'Call the police! They's a dead man in the park!'

Mr. Geoff, looking more than his sixty-odd years, peered out of the study. 'Girl, you trying to split my poor head? Quiet down out there!'

'Mr. Geoff, you got to come out here and see for yourself. He's dead — and he's a Holroyd, *just like you and me*!' She felt herself go faint all over with shock.

Never before this moment had she ever spoken of their kinship.

She must have looked woozy, for Miz Marilyn helped her sit down and brought a glass of water. Before heading for the phone she laid her hand softly on the black woman's shoulder, and tears came to her eyes.

'Dead?' Geoff burst out. 'A man dead in the Park? Is that what you told Marilyn just now?'

He turned toward the sitting room, where Marilyn had the telephone in her hand. 'My God, woman! *Don't* call the police!' he screamed.

She looked up. 'And *whom* do you want me to call?' she asked, her tone icy.

'Call Doc Jennings. He'll know what to do.'

Lutetia nodded in agreement. The old doctor had hidden more than one peccadillo in his years of tending to the Holroyds. He'd delivered her, and he'd tended to Mr. Geoff after he crashed his refurbished World War II bomber into those condominiums over in Redland. The survivors and families of those who died in the crash could have taken everything the family had, if they'd known the truth. Yes, a master at hiding things was Dr. Jennings.

Marilyn began to dial and Geoff almost ran to get back to his large array of bottles in the study.

'Lutetia.' Marilyn looked up from the phone. 'Where *is* the body?'

'T'ward this end of the Square, Miz Mar'lyn. Lyin' 'cross the path. It'd be mighty hard to miss 'im; he shows up from a right smart distance. You want me to go out and show you?'

Marilyn seemed to have regained control. 'No. That would cause the neighbors to notice. You let the doctor's car in, and we'll find a way to move . . . it . . . before the others are up. We must be careful about this. There are all sorts of things we don't need the police poking around in. We know that, don't we?'

Her tone was both cold and bitter, but Lutetia didn't much blame her. Marilyn Holroyd had inherited all the problems caused by her menfolk without a bit of the fun they'd had making them.

Lutetia sighed and went to sit beside the control panel for the gates. She heard Marilyn go upstairs, her feet dragging as if she were tired to death.

'Lord, help us,' Lutetia breathed, closing her eyes and leaning back in the tapestry chair. 'What's a goin' to happen next?'

SOPHIA ALLISON

Sophia woke early. Before opening her eyes she reached to feel if Tom was still safely there in bed, for last night had frightened her badly. She touched his warm skin and sighed with relief, but she could sleep no more.

Tom had gone out into the storm, dressed in dark clothing, his face an alien mask. Her only comfort had been the fact that the handgun was safely in *her* pocket. Yet something had changed her husband into someone she had never known, someone who slipped so easily into the night that she found it impossible to track his progress.

Amid the crack of thunder, the flash of lightning, and the pounding rain, she had waited for him to return, peering anxiously out of the windows, and stepping out onto the porch to try to find some sign that he was there. The individual who ran, at last, past the house toward the front gate had not been Tom. He was a different shape, in the glimpses afforded by the lightning.

Tom had returned within minutes of that sighting, soaked and pale, his eyes glazed with some memory she didn't really want to understand. She had rubbed him down after a hot bath, and put him to bed with a strong toddy inside him. He had dropped instantly into a sleep that seemed almost drugged.

What had happened last night? Had he killed that man who ran so desperately past her in the darkness? She understood enough of his military training to know that he would not require a weapon to do that. True, the stalker had threatened their son, but she was not ready to believe that meant he deserved death.

Shivering, despite the growing warmth of the pale morning light, Sophia prepared breakfast for herself and Ernest. Then she called Tom's secretary to tell her he would be late to work.

'I think he's coming down with

something, maybe a cold,' she told the woman. 'I'm letting him sleep in this morning.' She replaced the phone and turned to stare out through the front screen at the battered Park.

There was something there, lying on the path. Had a log floated up out of the river? She rejected the thought. The water had never come that high.

Then what *was* that dark form? It lay quite still, so it wasn't a misplaced alligator, driven out of its normal habitat.

Could it be a body?

Sophia shivered at the thought and touched her apron pocket where the automatic rested. Even as she stared, someone came into view from her own side of the Square — Cynthia Carruthers stood at the edge of the trees, enjoying the freshness of the morning.

Then she turned and obviously saw the same thing Sophia had been looking at. She stiffened, then, as Sophia watched in fascinated horror, she moved lightly *toward* the unidentifiable lump.

Her gasp was audible even from that considerable distance. Cynthia turned and ran blindly toward her own house, while Sophia, determined to discover the truth, came out to inspect the flotsam in the Park.

She wore only her slippers, but she disregarded the wet as she moved along the brick path toward the thing. She paused. She knew *what* it was, but not *who*. She didn't recognize the leaf-spattered features.

Would Cynthia call the police? Probably. But if not, she must call them now. Any delay on her part might cause suspicion. She ran to her own home and dialed 911.

'This is Mrs. Thomas Allison, Number Six, Holroyd Square. I just went out to see what damage the storm did in the Park, and I discovered a dead body there. Yes, quite dead. At least he is blue, which I feel must indicate that.'

The woman asked her to repeat the address and her name. Then, 'Did you see anything that might indicate what killed him?'

'I didn't touch him, but the water around him was pink. I should think it must be diluted blood. Do please send someone quickly . . . ' She ended the conversation abruptly and found Tom's gate opener on the hall table with his car keys. From her front porch, she activated the gates.

Then, calmly, she carried Ernest's breakfast up to him and came back down to eat something nourishing herself. This was not going to be an easy day, and she would need all her strength, she understood entirely too well.

CYNTHIA CARRUTHERS

Cynthia loved storms, but the damage they did to her beloved Park always distressed her. She had gone out very early to check on that, and what she found had her still quaking in her chair. She must call for help, she knew, but her frail body, never reliable under stress, had now let her down completely. She was simply unable to move far enough to reach the telephone.

Who was the dead man? Could it — could it possibly be the man who had threatened her and then taken her money?

Perhaps he had been struck by lightning, or a falling branch — by the hand of God, so to speak . . .

But she knew things rarely worked out that way in real life. She had seen a few tragedies in her time that had taught her the peril of living too close to those who were slaves to dangerous emotions.

That was why she had never considered any of the impassioned proposals she received in her youth. Her gifts were too precious to risk her far-from-robust body.

But she had never suspected her tame indulgences could be every bit as dangerous as the most reckless of lovers. She had paid the blackmail asked of her, and when the police discovered that, they might easily believe she had killed her tormentor. Was her unbroken peace here in this old house worth such fear as she felt now?

Cynthia rose, her bones feeling unreliable, and made her way to the desk where the telephone waited. At the very least, she must report her find. It would be suspicious of her not to do so.

SAM LEESON

The storm had wakened Sammy not long after he went to sleep. He liked watching lightning, so he got up and sat for a while at the window, and he had seen that man again in the erratic light, scooting over the wall from the Holroyds'. The dim figure still looked like his father, though his mother had reassured him he'd been way too young to remember anything about Daddy.

Later, as Sammy drooped at his post, the man returned, and this time he moved stiffly, as if he had hurt his arm. When he disappeared again over the wall, Sammy shrugged and reluctantly went back to bed.

He rose well before daylight, however, and dressed hurriedly. He wanted to see what, if anything, had transpired during the night.

He crossed the soggy lawn past flowers beaten down into the dirt. He moved through the front gate and across the street. Maybe the man had crossed over to the other side of the Square, once he left the Winchell property.

But he hadn't. Sammy spotted him almost immediately, lying in a puddle, staring up at the drooping branches that dripped water onto his bluish cheek. It was Daddy. Sammy might have been very small when he last looked into that face, but he remembered it well. Mama had been wrong. His father had returned, but now he was dead. Even a five-year-old could see that.

The boy turned and fled back home, but he did not wake Mama. Instead he stormed up the stairs to his grandfather's room.

'Grampa! Grampa! Daddy's dead in the Park!' he called through the door. 'Come help, Grampa!'

There came a grunt and a snort. Then his grandfather said, 'Come in, boy, come in. Now calm down, speak slowly, and tell me everything, just as it happened.'

Sammy did as he was told, then looked into his grandfather's face, hoping to see some solution to this dilemma.

'What should we do, Grampa?' he asked at last.

Arthur Winchell sat up slowly, twisted his skinny feet into his slippers, and pulled on his comfortable old bathrobe. 'Show me, boy,' he said. 'I can't decide till I know for sure it's who you think it is.'

They were standing just inside the front door, ready to step onto the porch when they saw Miz Carruthers come out of her house and go into the Park. 'She'll see 'im for sure,' Sammy muttered, disappointed that the official discovery wasn't to be his.

'I hope she does,' his grandfather replied. 'I don't want you to be on record as the one who found that body. I don't want you to have to go through what happens next in a situation like this. Let's just wait a bit and see what happens.'

After the pink-clad figure fled back across the street, Grampa nodded. 'That's that. There *is* a dead person there, all right, and we don't know for certain who it is. *Remember, Sammy, that you don't really know anything about this*. Nobody is likely to ask you any questions, and I don't have to report this, now that Miz Carruthers has seen it, but you keep your lip buttoned anyway.'

Something in his grandfather's expression made Sammy swallow hard and nod. Though he had looked forward to telling his tale to a bunch of policemen, Grampa seemed to think it wouldn't be any fun at all, and if there was anyone in this world that Sammy trusted, he was the one.

'I won't say a word, Grampa,' he promised. 'But I sure would like to know what's been going on.'

Arthur took his hand and led him back upstairs. 'Sammy, I would, too. But we have to keep our cool and hope we find out without asking. We don't want to make anything worse for your mother, now do we?'

Arthur went to his phone and punched in a number.

'I hate to bother you so early, Mrs. Shipp, but this is Arthur Winchell, and I need to speak to Wash, if you don't mind. No, I'll call back. How soon will he be out of the shower?

'Fine. I'll call back in about half an hour. Thank you, Mrs. Shipp. Goodbye, now.' And he hung up the phone with a sharp 'click.'

Shipp? Now who on earth is that? Sammy wondered as he went back into his room and closed his own door.

WASHINGTON SHIPP

Wash always sang spirituals in the shower — or even bits of operatic arias, when he could remember the words. Though he was too self-conscious to sing in public, as he soaped his mahogany skin, he reveled in the power of his voice.

His wife had trained as a concert pianist when she was younger, and she winced at bad notes as if she'd stepped on a grass burr. But she seemed to take pleasure in his long, musical interludes as much as he did, which was why, when he stepped into the kitchen, he was surprised to find her fidgeting.

'What's the matter, Jewel?' he asked. 'Did I hit a clunker?'

She shook her head. 'Mr. Arthur called, from the Square. He sounded mighty worried. I think you'd better call him back before you eat.'

Mr. Arthur was one of the rocks upon which Shipp's world was founded, and the thought that he was going on ninety was scary. He'd known the old man since he was a boy, tagging along with his Daddy to do the Winchell yard work.

There had been no electronic gates then, just the wall and a buzzer to be pushed for somebody to let you in. The Winchells were the only folks on the Square that his Daddy worked for, and Wash remembered clearly, sitting in their big bright kitchen eating cookies and drinking milk, while his Daddy and Mr. Arthur argued politics or books or music.

The Winchells were the only dedicated opera lovers on the Square, and it had been Mr. Arthur who arranged for Wash to win a music scholarship. But Wash was afflicted with a stage fright so severe he had never been able to conquer it. That ended his musical career, but Mr. Arthur had loaned him the money to continue school anyway.

His education had been wonderful. He majored in criminal justice, which got him onto the Templeton police force as one of the earliest black officers. He had used his abilities so well that he now carried the title of Assistant Police Chief.

When Chief Rawlinson retired next year, which his state of health almost guaranteed, Wash had been promised his job.

He sipped at a cup of coffee while he punched in Arthur's private phone number. The voice at the other end sounded wavy and cracked.

'Wash, here, Mr. Arthur. Jewel tells me you called. What can I do for you?'

'Wash, there's something badly wrong in the Square.' Wash could tell the old man wasn't exaggerating. 'Your station may have received a 911 call a while ago. I just saw Miss Carruthers go running out of the Park, heading for her house, and she looked scared to death. I'm sure she called at once.'

'But we're not allowed into the Square,' Wash interjected. 'Mr. Geoff has never in his life called us in, no matter what the problem. There'd be hell to pay if we showed up there without *his* permission.'

'I think there's already hell to pay,

Wash. I went out and looked hard over there. Seemed as if I could see something that looked entirely too much like a dead body lying on the path through the Park.

'I don't mean to sound insistent Wash, but if we've got to have the law out here, I'd much rather it'd be you and some of the men you trust. We're set in our ways here, and having strangers nosing around will make a lot of people mighty nervous.'

Wash was gripping the phone entirely too tightly in his big black hand. A body in the Square? He wouldn't have been more surprised if he'd been told the sun had risen in the west that morning. The Square and dead bodies, other than properly coffined ones, just didn't co-exist in the same world.

'I'll check with the station, Mr. Arthur. Then I'll be there as quick as I can. You . . . you take care, hear?'

He gulped down the rest of his coffee and turned to Jewel. 'I won't have time to eat. There's something wrong over there, and I need to move fast. Geoff Holroyd owns half the city commission. We can't afford to take any chances we don't have to.'

She nodded as she folded a fried egg and two pieces of bacon between two slices of buttered toast. 'You eat this on the way. You don't want to have any more low blood sugar problems.'

He took the napkin-wrapped sandwich and bent to kiss her coppery cheek.

'Yes, ma'am, I will,' he promised. Then he was on his way.

Templeton, like many towns in East Texas, was still struggling in the twentieth century while the rest of the world was getting accustomed to the twenty-first. The schools had been integrated for decades, but the city government had only recently come to grips with representing the twenty-five percent of the population that was black, and another ten percent that was Hispanic.

Those families who had run things forever, fought a long delaying action, but when at last the old guard was gone, the sons and grandsons of the old regime had bitten the bullet. There was a black county commissioner, and both a black and a Hispanic city commissioner.

Five years ago they had promoted Washington Shipp to Assistant Police Chief, and since then he had added several promising black graduates from the local state university's criminal justice program to his team. Although most of the force, including the chief, were sound, rational people, there were others who were, in his opinion, rock-solid idiots.

Wash shivered at the idea of any of the few rednecks on the force waltzing into the Square and trying to push those quiet but highly influential people around. Tom Allison, for instance, was a prominent lawyer with ties to D.C. He'd be all over them if somebody screwed up.

Turning into the parking lot at the station, Wash sat for a moment, wiping his buttery fingers on the napkin. This was not going to be a good day; he could see that already.

He stopped Sharon, the night dispatcher, in the hall. 'Have we gotten any kind of emergency call from the Square?'

She nodded. 'About twenty minutes ago. Dan Gerrell should be there by now.'

Wash turned back toward his car. 'Thanks, Sharon. But damnit, anyway.' Her chuckle of understanding followed him out to the parking lot. Gerrell was one of the few idiots on the force. Just what he had feared.

* * *

The iron grillwork gates off Richmond stood open. As Wash pulled in front of the Winchell place, he took in the multiple squad and EMT vehicles with their red lights flashing, parked helter-skelter around the Square. He could see people standing about on their front porches, talking softly among themselves and watching the confusion taking place in their normally quiet enclosure.

He saw Mrs. Allison as he walked through the gates, and nodded to her politely. She started out to meet him, but paused.

'I'll come back and let y'all know what's going on just as soon as I can, Miz Allison,' he called out to her.

'Oh, I already know about it, Mr.

Shipp. I was the first to call in, I think, though it might have been Cynthia. We saw . . . *it* . . . at about the same time.'

'Mr. Winchell called me at home,' he said. 'I'd better get over there and make sure those fellows don't mess anything up.'

He saw yellow tape neatly surrounding what was obviously a crime scene — which meant only one thing — there really was a dead body in the Park. Gerrell was standing, red-faced, in front of the Winchell place, arms gesticulating wildly as he talked with Arthur, who looked to Wash even more frail than he had sounded on the phone.

Geoff Holroyd was chugging toward them with the determination of an army tank. If that combination of super-egos and alcohol-fueled tempers collided, it wouldn't be pretty. Wash broke into a run.

'Hey . . . Gerrell,' he panted, screeching to a halt. 'Have you called the Judge yet?'

'Nope. But I've got men going over every square inch, looking for clues.' The ruddy-faced Gerrell looked smug.

'That's fine, but I'll need to see the

body myself, and you need to call the JP pronto. You know we can't move him until he's pronounced dead, you know.'

'If I don't know a dead man by now . . . ' Gerrell began huffily.

Wash interrupted him. 'That don't matter. The law says he can't be moved until the JP confirms he's dead. Now make that call while I check out the site. You'd better go in and sit down, Mr. Arthur, you look a bit pale. I'll be along to see you in a little bit.'

He turned to intercept Geoff's headlong charge. 'There you are, Colonel Holroyd. Do you want to go over there with me to see what's happened? Seeing as how you're the boss man here, I think that would be appropriate.'

And just as easily as that, he had diverted the three most dangerous elements in different directions, thus preventing critical mass from occurring just yet. One of Wash's most valuable and unrecognized skills was that of short-circuiting potential problems.

With Holroyd sputtering along behind him, he ducked through the crepe myrtles to gain the crooked brick path. Together they moved toward a cluster of men examining the ground. Two were staring down at the leaf-littered shape on the walk, their cameras still in their hands, though they had obviously finished taking pictures so that the body could be moved.

'Been dead most of the night,' Jim Benton said as Wash joined him. 'You can see where the blood has washed off him. He doesn't look a bit familiar to me. You know him?'

Wash lifted the branch that obscured the cold features and stared down into the pale eye cocked upward toward the treetops. He looked closely at the shape of the face, the curve of the brow, the angle of the jaw.

'Colonel Holroyd, would you look at this man?' he asked. 'See anything . . . familiar?'

Geoff bent over the body. He stiffened for a moment then looked up at Wash.

'There's a family resemblance, isn't there? Something about the jaw line. That doesn't mean much around Templeton, of course. I've got tons of cousins . . . maybe even some half-brothers and sisters between here and the county line. My Daddy got around a bit, as you probably know.'

Wash nodded. 'Seemed to be some sort of family likeness to me.' He glanced toward the Holroyd drive in surprise. 'I see Doc Jennings is here. Somebody sick?' he asked.

'Marilyn got all upset when the police cars came screaming into the Square,' Geoff acknowledged. 'I was worried about her, so I called Dr. Jennings to check on her.'

Wash had already figured that was the case. But he also had a strong hunch that Jennings had been covering up Holroyd misdeeds for decades. 'Nobody in your house saw this fellow then?' he asked.

Geoff gazed back at him blankly. 'Not to my knowledge,' he said, and Wash knew instantly that he was lying through his teeth.

Another car came into the Square delivering Judge Finley, who quickly joined the small group gathered at the crime scene.

'Go on back and look after Miz Marilyn,' Wash urged Geoff. 'I'll take care of everything here; then I'll come on in and talk about this with y'all before I leave.'

The judge looked around the area carefully, bent over the body, felt about the cyanotic face with a latex-gloved hand then stood. 'I officially declare this man to be dead under suspicious circumstances,' he stated formally. 'You may remove the body to the morgue for further examination.'

'Hold on,' Wash instructed his men. 'I need to search the body myself before we move it.' He pulled latex gloves from his pocket, stretched them onto his big hands, and with the aid of his officers, carefully turned the body onto its back.

He felt inside the pocket of the dark sweatshirt, but it was empty. Then he worked his hands into the pants pockets. There was nothing there, either. But the wide belt seemed unusually thicker than normal. He unbuckled it and slipped it free. It was a money belt, neatly lined with twenty-dollar bills. A *lot* of money,

Wash realized, as he counted it out. At one end there was a small blue notebook.

Wash carefully sealed the contents of the belt into a plastic bag, then coiled the belt and sealed it into another bag. 'I'm putting my stickers over these bags, Mr. Findley,' he said to the JP. 'Would you initial it? Here, where I've signed it . . . '

The judge readily complied then they all stood aside as the ambulance moved in. Once the corpse was zipped into a body bag and removed, Wash looked carefully at the soaked ground where it had lain. He scooped up a vial of the pink rainwater and sealed it also, holding it out for Finley's initials.

A storm like that would have washed away any tracks or other signs of the assailant. The fatal blow, he judged, had come from behind. The gunshot wound in the arm was probably not the cause of death.

So why, he wondered, would someone have gone to the trouble to shoot a man first then bludgeon him to death? Or had he hit him first? No, he acknowledged grudgingly. The victim probably would not have lost that much blood from a post mortem gunshot wound.

Given the private natures of those living in the Square, unless some other evidence emerged linking one of them to the crime, it would more than likely go unsolved. Wash knew only too well the political pressure that had prevented other, less grievous crimes from being resolved.

He moved toward the Winchell house for his talk with Mr. Arthur, hoping there was something in the little book that might give him a clue. That much money was suspicious in itself. Most honest people kept their assets safely locked away in a bank. The more unsavory types kept their funds on their persons, in case they had to leave in a hurry.

So who was this dead man? How had he gotten into the Square? Why had someone killed him and left him there, out in the open, where the body could be readily discovered?

As he rang the Winchell doorbell, he pondered the fact with both sadness and resignation that he might never now find the answers to these questions.

ARTHUR MELLINGHAM WINCHELL

Time moved slowly, while Arthur waited for Wash's return.

He rather resented his self-imposed retreat from the crime scene. No matter how shaky his health might be, he repeatedly crept downstairs, ignoring his daughter's entreaties that he go back up to his room and 'have a lie down' until Mr. Wash should be ready for him. Sammy was there, too, maintaining an uncharacteristic and stoical silence. When Arthur sank into the deep parlor recliner, the boy crept close to his side and perched on the footstool beside him, saying nothing.

Arthur knew the boy was wondering if that really *was* his father. And would anyone out there recognize him? Had anyone in the Square, except for this family, known him well since he became an adult?

Margaret turned on the television, but Arthur had Sammy shut it off again. The raucous sound set him on edge, and he felt an unfamiliar urgency to control everything: his nerves, his voice, and his reactions.

Wash Shipp, he knew, was a highly intelligent crime-solver. It would be difficult to fool him, which was one reason Arthur had refused to go out and confirm the identity of the body. He hadn't seen it except from a distance, so he had no idea if Sammy was correct. What he might *suspect,* though, was irrelevant, and the statement of a five-year-old would carry little or no weight with the minions of the law.

At last a heavy footstep sounded on the porch. Arthur waited impatiently for Margaret to answer the ring. It wouldn't do to seem too anxious. 'You go on upstairs,' he told Sammy. 'You don't want to get mixed up in this thing.'

The boy's obedience, without question or argument, told Arthur more than anything else that the corpse in the Park was most likely his dead son-in-law.

Margaret had been properly informed of Saul's accidental death, the insurance was paid without protest, and the company had made no problem about the benefits, but in some way, Arthur felt sure, Leeson had managed to slip through the cracks, even of death itself.

Wash took off his cap and laid it on the hall table before entering the parlor. 'Mr. Arthur,' he said, choosing a stout-looking chair before risking his considerable weight to it. 'We've definitely got a dead body out there. It was probably murder, though the gunshot wound was not, I feel sure, the cause of death. He was struck from behind, at an angle, by someone wielding either a pipe or a very solid stick or board.'

Wash shifted his feet as he looked into Arthur's eyes. 'Colonel Holroyd agrees he's got a look about him that reminds us of the Holroyds. You know anybody like that?'

'Too many,' Arthur sighed. 'There's Lutetia, for instance, who keeps house for

Geoff and his sister. There's Cole Watters who runs the dry-cleaning place. And a dozen more, all most likely the result of Jesse Holroyd and his father — and his son — if you want to know the truth — tomcattin' around.'

'Didn't your daughter marry Geoff Holroyd's cousin?' Wash asked, his voice betraying no special emphasis.

'Yes, she did. Saul Leeson was the grandson of Jesse's sister Kate. He would be — let's see, if he were still alive he'd be about forty-eight or thereabouts. But he was killed in the Far East about three years ago. That was when my daughter and her kids moved in here with me.' Arthur hoped his voice and his manner emphasized Saul was a definitely deceased son-in-law.

'So he's dead? I thought Miz Margaret might be divorced. Seems to me I recall Mr. Leeson had a pretty vile temper . . . '

Wash was speaking carefully, which warned Arthur to do the same. He knew Wash would more than likely head back to his office to run down everything the computer system could tell him about all the inhabitants of the Square, including the dead ones. Best not say anything that later could be disproved.

'He *was* a rotter, and he treated my daughter abominably,' Arthur admitted. 'If he came back from the dead and I was able, I'd send him back there as fast as possible. But, I haven't heard a thing about him since the funeral. Margaret never mentions him, and what little the boys remember doesn't amount to a hill of beans.' There, that should be cagey enough.

Wash nodded. 'All the same, you think you might be willing to come down to the morgue and take a look at the body?' he asked. 'I've got to ask someone from every house on the Square to do that, and I purely hate to ask your daughter to do it.'

Arthur hated lying with a passion, but he could do nothing but agree. Anything else would seem suspicious. And he couldn't risk letting Maggie do it. She wasn't someone who hid her feelings at all well. If it *was* Saul, she'd betray the fact by her expression.

'Thank you, Mr. Arthur,' Wash said, leaning to shake hands before turning toward the door. 'I've got to go see some more people now. There's going to be a regular parade in and out of here, before this thing is done. Just call me when you're ready and I'll come get you myself.'

Arthur watched him go down the walk with mixed feelings. Wash was a credit to him, true, but he was also a danger, if the body proved to be Saul. And that was something he intended to find out, right now.

He limped back where Margaret was cleaning up after getting the boys fed. She turned in surprise, for her father seldom entered the kitchen.

'We need to talk,' he said, taking a seat on one of the wooden kitchen chairs. 'I'm sure you heard what Wash was saying. You know what was found in the Park this morning.

'So tell me the truth. Has there been anything at all that might make you think Saul might still be alive?' To his dismay she froze for a moment, her hands gripping the edge of the sink so hard her knuckles turned pale.

When she turned, he already knew the answer. 'So he *is* alive, or was. I greatly fear his was the body they found this morning. You've got to tell me the truth now, Maggie. Why on earth did you keep it a secret?'

She dropped heavily onto the chair beside his, her hands twisting in her lap. 'He showed up here about a year after they told me he died,' she whispered. 'I told him I didn't want him back.

'But he threatened to come back anyway, pretending to be brain-damaged, and be a burden on me for the rest of his life. I paid him everything I could scrounge up, Papa. And it was worth it!' Her eyes were rimmed with red, but they held more determination than he'd ever believed his timid daughter possessed.

'Did *you* kill him?' asked Arthur.

'I wanted to,' she whispered. 'But I swear I didn't.'

And, to his great relief, Arthur found her believable.

WASHINGTON SHIPP

Wash made the rounds of the Square, questioning all the tenants, as well as the Holroyds.

Cynthia Carruthers had nearly fainted when he asked her to look at the body, once the morgue had it ready.

Garth Overedge had seemed ill at ease as well. His wife, also pale and distracted, had said nothing, though she fidgeted with the ruffle on her blouse while listening to them talk.

Sophia Allison seemed the least nervous of all of them. Yes, she had made the 911 call after going to see what had frightened her neighbor. No, she had not recognized the man, though she didn't examine the body closely. No, her husband had not gone out last night. The storm was bad, and he had not been feeling well. In fact, he was still in bed with a slight fever. She intended on calling the doctor, once things settled down.

Wash could tell she was hiding something, but this had been true of all the tenants in the Square. Every single one of them seemed to be sitting on something too dangerous to mention, but it was his firm belief that only in fictional mysteries did an entire group conspire to kill a victim.

If he could learn the man's identity, that would go a long way towards confirming what — or who — had killed him. The little notebook he had retrieved from the money belt must be an important piece of evidence. But what did it mean?

* * *

Templeton was on East Texas time, so it was noon the next day before the morgue called to say the body was ready for viewing. Wash sent a car for the witnesses who had agreed to inspect the corpse, and he stayed clear of the entire matter.

He intended to examine the notebook thoroughly, and that was quite enough to keep him busy for the day.

The name scrawled just inside the front cover was 'Earl Branson,' which meant nothing to him, and did not seem to be associated with anyone in the case. However, the subsequent pages were more than illuminating. One was devoted entirely to the Holroyds. Carefully noted were the thefts of several valuable pieces from their house, along with prices received for their sale. The tidy sum of something just over seven thousand dollars was tallied up there.

Also there were several statements followed by question marks, as if the writer had suspicions without evidence about several matters. The first question posed was: 'G drunk when cr.? Doc Jennings cu?' Which was plain enough. Everyone knew about that terrible plane crash, and everyone also knew Geoff Holroyd was a drunk. Dr. Jennings, in spite of his good reputation, had been associated with the Holroyd family clear back to his grandfather's time. If anyone could cover up such a mess, it would be him.

The next note puzzled him. 'J? Maybe M?' That would require longer consideration. When he moved to the next page, his eyes widened in surprise. The reason for Milton Thomas Martin's very short military career was divulged in great detail. At the end of the page there was a column of spaces, in the first box of which the sum of $5,000 was neatly printed.

'So he was a blackmailer!' Wash muttered. 'That explains a lot.'

The Allison page contained a single name: 'Ernest.' 'Helpless' was written directly after that. Then: 'Internet?' There was no sum listed in the boxed column that ended the page. But that still sounded like possible extortion.

Cynthia Carruthers came next. 'Something illegal goin' on? Blinds always closed w/lights on. A/C on there/off in rest of house. Weak sister.' There was another $5,000 listed on this page.

So Miz Carruthers might be doing something fishy in her back room that she didn't want known. Wash was very doubtful it was anything illegal, but she could be desperate enough to do something drastic. Still, those fragile arms couldn't swing a weighted pipe hard enough to kill a man. Or could they?

'Overedge. Beats wife and kids. Threaten to inform?'

That was self-explanatory, and Wash decided to have a talk with the man. At the bottom of the page was listed 'C. W. Gun, $8,000.00.' Was it a Civil War weapon that he had stolen or had he been offered it as some sort of payment?

'E. Holt fooling around? Make O.H. pay.'

Now that was interesting! Only days before old Olivia Holt at Number Five had been taken away to the psych ward, after trying to have her now married daughter committed for mental observation. Evidently this sonofabitch had sent some kind of message that riled Olivia Holt to the point at which she lost control.

There was no sum listed there either.

The Winchell page held only a single

word: 'Margaret.' At its bottom were several neat columns of figures adding up to thousands of dollars, evidently over several years.

Wash sank back into his office chair. Not a house on the Square, seemingly, failed to hold someone who had good reason to kill the man who owned this notebook. If Margaret Leeson had paid so much for so long, it was likely this man meant something to her. Could it be that Saul Leeson had not died several years ago, as Arthur had claimed?

Wash requested all available information on the man, and the computer began to access the databases. Before tomorrow he would know a lot more than he did now.

WASHINGTON SHIPP

If there was anything to be thankful for, Wash knew, it was that the body had turned up on a Monday. Otherwise, nobody would have been available locally to give permission for the lines of inquiry he needed to pursue. Chief Rawlinson would have been resting at home, not to be disturbed, and the judge likely would have been in Austin attending some meeting or other. Permission to go over the notebook for clues would have been hard to come by. As it was, however, he now knew what trails to follow up, and he set Suzy, his resident computer genius, to work on it. She had a magic touch and would, he knew, come up with what he needed at the speed of light.

He loved to watch the faces of the assorted rednecks on the force as they watched Suzy make that computer sit up and whistle Dixie. They didn't really intend to be bigots, he knew. They just didn't know what to expect from a black woman. Suzy tended to unsettle their wits, big-time.

Meanwhile, he kept track of the Square residents who visited the morgue. In addition to one of his officers, he made sure the local undertaker, Henry Furlong was in attendance. It never hurt to have two sets of eyes watching.

'I'm glad you called, Wash,' Henry said. 'I was about to contact you. There's a bit of damage to the corpse you might want to take a look at. Looks like somebody nearly broke his shoulder a couple of days ago. The bruises are significant.'

'Now that's mighty interesting,' Wash replied. 'I'll be right over.'

Once he had examined the body he ordered pictures taken of the old injury. 'That was either one unlucky dude, or he went around asking for trouble,' he mused, staring down at the vivid bruises.

'To get hit that hard, then before those bruises have faded, to get shot, *then,* on top of all that, to have your neck broken, seems to indicate a pretty active lifestyle, don't you think?' He looked up into Henry's pale gray eyes.

The undertaker chuckled. 'This was not a popular man, in my judgment, and I would bet a considerable sum on that. My guess is that he's better off dead than alive, but that's not my call, of course . . .

'No, you law folks are gonna have to poke around and find the poor sucker who killed him, whatever good reason he might have had for doing it, and then get him all tried and convicted and maybe even put to sleep permanently.' Furlong sighed. 'If I were the police, which thank God I'm not, I'd be lookin' to hand the killer a medal, and that wouldn't be popular with the powers that be.'

'Don't think that didn't occur to me,' Wash muttered. 'I had the same problem when that child molester walked last year; I almost resigned it upset me so much.'

He and Henry had been friends for years, and Wash knew they felt much the same. Sometimes this job was a pure pain, and this looked like one of those instances. That body might look pitiful, but the curl of the lip and the slant of the brows, gave it the look of someone willful and dangerous, even in death.

And there was something about the shape of the shoulder bruise that puzzled Wash. It looked — by golly, it looked almost like the profile of a very small face! He quickly showed the photographer what he wanted then stood back as the camera clicked away. Wash was still wondering if their corpse was the supposedly dead Saul Leeson. By the time he returned to the office, Suzy should have the results from the fingerprint search. Even if the dead man's information had been relegated to some sort of inactive file, there should be some record still available, somewhere.

Could Arthur Winchell have encountered the supposedly deceased Saul and taken a hand to protect his daughter? No. picturing the old man's skinny frame, fragile bones, and shaky stance, Wash sincerely doubted it.

And Margaret probably would have stopped her father from going out in the kind of storm that had shaken Templeton on Sunday night. She was a determined woman, he knew, no matter if she seemed quiet and subdued.

'*I don't think it's Mr. Arthur*,' he admitted aloud, turning into his parking space at the station. '*Anybody else maybe, but not him*.'

Once in his office, he began to sort through all the relevant records Suzy had piled onto his desk. It was a forbidding stack of paper, but he sighed and began leafing through it, making notes from time to time and setting aside a sheet now and again for further investigation.

He made seven different stacks, one for each of the houses on the Square. Then he noted the dead man's comments, taken from the little book, onto file cards and set those on top of each stack. It might not answer any questions, but at least it was tidy, and was a step toward solving this troubling case.

Chief Rawlinson's buzzer sounded, and he pulled himself to his feet. When the Chief called, he went. The old man was making few demands on him these days, but he kept a shrewd eye on what went on in the department. Now he must be itching with curiosity over the progress being made on this unusual murder.

The chief was hunched in the huge leather chair behind his desk, staring out over a large, but neat, desk. He was waiting out his time to be eligible for his pension, and everyone, from members of the city council to all those under his command, conspired daily to make things easy for him without betraying the fact that they knew he was too ill to do much work.

'Come in, Wash,' Rawlinson said, shifting his weight uneasily. His voice was almost breathless, instead of the gruff rumble it had been just a few years before. 'Tell me about this Holroyd business in the Square. Not a good thing, you know. Not a good thing at all.'

Wash knew that all too well, but he sat in a chair across the desk from his superior and went through, in painstaking detail, the sequence of events that had begun earlier that morning. 'I've sent the body's prints to the FBI. Just exactly what we'll do if this turns out to be Saul

Leeson, a man who's supposed to be dead, is something I haven't quite figured out yet.'

Rawlinson leaned forward and leaned on the worn oak of his desktop. 'Ya' know . . . it wouldn't surprise me a bit,' he wheezed. 'Ya' see, I *knew* Saul. You were still in college when he married Maggie Winchell. He hadn't been back to Templeton since he was a kid, but he hung around here for the better part of a year while he was a'courtin' her.

'Bein' a cousin of the Holroyds gave him a lot of backing. Didn't go around the Square much though, I noticed. He'd pick Maggie up in front of the gates, instead of goin' up to the house.

'Nobody was too surprised when she up and married him. I guess she was just a homely little girl who decided she'd never have a better chance of landin' a husband. She'd have been better off stayin' single, if I sized that fellow up right . . . '

Wash nodded. 'Even his corpse looks like a hard case. The notes he made in that little book pretty well show he was not only a thief, but a blackmailer and would-be extortionist, to boot. Does that fit your assessment of ol' Saul?'

'Might. Though I never actually *saw* him do anything illegal. Still, once in a long while, Arthur and I would meet at meetings or such, I thought he looked a might grim when I asked about how his daughter and her new husband were gettin' on.'

'There's others in the Square who might have had motives for doing him in,' Wash said, handing the small volume to the older man. 'You might want to just look through that and let me know what you think. Motive is the unknown factor in this mess, and we've got more suspects than a dog has fleas.'

The chief took the little book in trembling, blue-veined fingers, but instead of glancing at it, stared wearily from dark-ringed eyes at Wash. He seemed particularly depressed. 'Wash, this is going to be a bitch. Unless you can find some outsider who managed to get into the Square and kill whoever that may be, you're going to get backlash like you never felt before.' He gave a sigh that was half a groan.

'I had a case like this some twenty years ago, when *I* was Assistant Chief. One of those rich guys over in the Hills strangled his wife. Her scratches were on his wrists and his skin was under her fingernails, for God's sake, and the sonofabitch walked. The combination of old money and generations of political favors is something the best cop in the world can't beat.'

Wash felt sick at heart. 'You mean it never even went to trial?'

'The District Attorney instructed the Grand Jury to dismiss him. That poor woman got buried so fast it would make your head swim, and ten days later the grieving widower married the children's nanny. I bucked and snorted like a yearling mule, but the old Chief knew what was going to happen. He warned me, from the first, that no matter how hard I worked, no matter what proof there was, the case was going nowhere. And it didn't.'

Wash was born and raised in Temple County, so he pretty much understood how things worked. Still, even his long years in the profession had not prepared him for the way things were done in the courthouse at Templeton.

If he found the killer and had to stand back and watch him go free it was going to bother him a lot. From the look in Rawlinson's faded eyes, he knew it had bothered the chief a lot, too, over the years.

'I still have to go through with the investigation,' he said finally. 'Even if it does no good at all. I couldn't live with myself if I just let it go.' Rising, Wash turned toward the door.

'I know you've got to do what you got to do, Wash. I had to, too, when I was your age. But watch your back, you hear? Some of these folks you're dealing with don't have consideration for anybody outside their little bunch. And you're black, of course. That won't help you one little bit with most of them. Arthur Winchell is the only really unbiased person in the Square, but I don't know how much influence he still has these days.'

Nodding in resignation, Wash left the chief's office and returned to his own, where he found Suzy, shifting impatiently from foot to foot. 'We got 'im!' she whispered, when they were behind the closed door. 'It *is* Saul Leeson! His death was reported two-and-a-half years ago, in Cambodia, of all places!'

It was what Wash had suspected from the beginning. Who else but Saul Leeson, who had frequented the Square as a child, would have known how to spy on the inhabitants without raising an alarm? Who else could have traipsed in and out of their houses with all the knowledge he needed of layouts and the people living there? Not to mention the pricey old family heirlooms that the adult Saul would know how to fence.

'Good work, Suzy,' he said. 'Gives us something to get our teeth into, if nothing else. Now I'm going to go ask Henry if anyone has been willing to identify the body yet.'

He arrived at the morgue just as a car pulled up to let Arthur Winchell out. The old man looked almost as blue as the body he was being asked to identify, and Wash rushed to take his arm and help him toddle up the wheelchair ramp.

'Thank you, Wash,' Arthur wheezed. 'You know, I'm not lookin' forward to this a damn bit.'

'Don't blame you, Mr. Arthur. I'll go in with you, if you want. I need to speak to Henry, anyway.'

Together they moved into the dim reception area. Wash was reminded entirely too much of his own mortality. 'Back here,' twittered Henry's assistant, moving silently ahead of them to the small room where the corpse was now awaiting its final disposition.

Arthur staggered at first, but pulled himself erect and marched determinedly to the table. Wash, holding his elbow, kept pace with the old fellow as he moved to stand beside the sheeted shape.

Henry pulled aside the cloth covering the still face. 'Here, Mr. Arthur,' he said gently. 'See if you can identify this man.'

Arthur adjusted his glasses and bent slightly to look down at the waxen features. He shuddered, which Wash felt through the elbow he held. When he straightened he gave a sigh and turned to Wash.

'This is my son-in-law, Saul Leeson, who was reported to have died in a traffic accident in Cambodia nearly three years ago.'

Henry pulled up a chair, just in time to keep Arthur from sinking to the floor. Wash helped ease him down while Henry sent his assistant after a shot of whiskey. The stimulant brought a bit of color back into Arthur's thin cheeks and steadied his quivering body. As soon as he was able, Winchell looked up at Wash and asked, 'So what do we do now?'

And that was indeed a relevant question, from many angles and perspectives.

CYNTHIA CARRUTHERS

Cynthia spent the morning shivering and weeping. Never had she faced such a terrible situation in the Square, where Mama and Papa had lived without any problem for years. And before that, her grandparents had been equally untroubled. What had happened to their serene world? First she was blackmailed, which distasteful as it was, was still something she could handle. Murder, however, was something she had never encountered. Even during her education in Paris, she had avoided the daily press and its lurid details of violence.

She was so distraught that she took out a bottle of French brandy and poured herself a small helping in one of the crystal snifters. Sitting in her deep chair, with the draperies closed against the goings on in the Park across the way, she had sipped slowly and tried to settle her crumbling nerves.

By late afternoon, Cynthia had come to a decision. What was so terrible about moving? People did it every day in the world. She had enough money to keep her. She would find a house or, she thought suddenly with excitement, a *condominium,* with space for her lifetime of accumulations, and a security guard on duty — day and night — to protect them.

She began leafing through the Yellow Pages for moving companies, realizing that she must ask for references. There were valuable antiques among her possessions. China and crystal, porcelain, Delftware, Lalique . . . Milton Martin was not the only person on the Square with a small fortune in family treasures.

An even more daring thought suddenly occurred to her. Why move all this useless stuff? She had no children, only some distant cousins she hardly knew. Why should she not turn some of her things into cash, as she knew Milton had? His cousin, she knew, had handled the sale. Perhaps he would be willing to do the same for her.

At once, before she could change her mind, Cynthia called Milton and asked for his cousin's number. She smiled wryly at the amazement in the man's voice. It was obvious he had never considered the possibility that *she* might do something unexpected herself. As soon as she finished with him, she called his cousin.

A voice answered the ring. 'Henderson Antiques. May I help you?'

For a moment, Cynthia's nerve failed her. Did she really want to do this? Could she bear to part with her grandmother's Haviland or her mother's lusterware? They were part of her — the plates and cups, the pink glow emanating from shaded lamps.

'*I am forty-seven years old*,' she said aloud. '*I have no one to leave this to. Why should I not put it to good use?*'

'I beg your pardon?' The disembodied voice sounded puzzled.

'And I beg yours,' Cynthia said. 'Just musing aloud. I need to speak with Ronald Henderson. My neighbor, Milton Martin, has recommended him to me as a good agent for selling my family heirlooms.'

The voice warmed immediately. 'I'm Mr. Henderson. I will be delighted to help you, Mrs . . . ?'

'*Miss* Carruthers. Cynthia Carruthers. Number Two, Holroyd Square . . . '

Before she had quite finished, Henderson interrupted. 'I know you by reputation, Miss Carruthers. Milton has spoken of you. I suspect you saw us putting together some of his antiques for sale and thought you might do the same?'

'I intend to move,' she said, finding the bald statement liberating. 'There is no use in packing and moving such fragile things, when there will probably be no room for them in the new place. I have no heirs who might appreciate the things, and it occurred to me that moving them is a big waste of time.'

'We're almost ready to close,' Henderson said. 'Would you like for me to come over now for a preliminary examination of the items you might want to sell?'

Was that the sound of a car stopping before her gate? Cynthia said hurriedly,

'No. Not tonight. I have . . . guests. But tomorrow, if you might manage that, would be fine. Just call before you come. I am . . . I am in the book.'

She replaced the telephone quickly and darted to the window overlooking the porch. She held back a fold and peeked out; a very large shape was climbing her front steps, dark and forbidding as a storm cloud. It was that black policeman, Arthur Winchell's pet. Why could it not have been Chief Rawlinson, who had known her father and who would be properly in awe of the Carruthers name? She had observed Wash Shipp's career over the years, and she feared *he* was awed by nothing. She trembled as she crept toward the door and waited for the bell to ring.

How should she handle this? Then, for the first time since she left for Paris in the teeth of parental fury, Cynthia felt a surge of courage. She would just tell the truth. After all, she had done nothing wrong. She could see that now.

She pulled open the heavy door, letting in a gust of air, and glued a determined smile to her quivering lips. 'Chief Shipp, isn't it? I am glad you came back. I have something I must tell you.'

He looked somewhat taken aback, but he came in, removing his cap and carefully laying it on the hall table. 'I, also, have something to tell *you*, Miss Carruthers. Maybe I'd better get mine told first. Then we can discuss your information.'

She nodded and led him into the parlor, where she bravely flung open the draperies. Once they were facing each other, with Wash perched uncomfortably on a delicate velvet-upholstered chair, she leaned forward in anticipation of what news he might offer.

'Arthur Winchell has identified the dead man as his son-in-law, Saul Leeson.' Whatever she had expected, it *certainly* had not been that! She looked up into his warm brown eyes, and recognized, for the first time, she realized, the man's watchful intelligence.

'My God!' she exclaimed, forgetting all propriety. 'I thought he was dead!'

Shipp smiled and relaxed a bit. 'So did

most everyone else, it seems. But he wasn't. He has been engaged in theft and blackmail involving almost every family on the Square. Now — what was it *you* wanted to tell me?'

'Including me,' she said, her voice very small. 'I paid that man five thousand dollars a few days back, because he hinted that he knows what I . . . what I do in my back room. My study.'

'Miz Carruthers, what on earth could a nice lady like you do in your back study that would be bad enough to make you pay blackmail?' Shipp asked.

'Not bad!' she objected. 'Oh no, not bad — or illegal. But it . . . it breaks my . . . my lease.' She felt suddenly a little ill. Standing quickly, she gestured toward the back of the house.

'I might as well show you. I have decided I am going to move anyway. Nothing is worth the kind of misery and stress I have suffered over this.' She led the way down the hall and unlocked the study door.

The study was, as usual, quiet and orderly; when she flipped the switch, the lily-shaped globes of the overhead lamps filled the room with a soft, natural light. Her easel held a delicate incomplete sketch on heavy paper. Finished watercolors hung around the walls, some matted and framed, all betraying the forbidden legend: 'work for pay.'

Shipp gazed about, at first puzzled — then amazed — as he moved about the room, looking closely at the works she was preparing for her next showing.

He bent to examine the signature in the corner of her newest work, *Stained Glass Amaryllis*. Turning, he said in awe, '*You* are Cyd! For heaven's sake, Miz Carruthers, why have you hidden your work away like this? This is . . . it's simply wonderful.

'I read that art magazine this month, the one with the interview with what's-his-name, saying *you* were one of the best-known male artists of our time!' Wash Shipp began to laugh, the deep boom of his voice reminding her that he was a singer himself. Evidently he appreciated art as much as he did music.

'I so hated to give up my home,' she whispered. 'Geoff wants to get everybody on the old leases out, so he can collect much higher rents. I was sure he'd use my work as an excuse to get rid of me. But now I'm going to get rid of myself, Mr. Shipp. Life is way too short to live in fear of discovery.'

'I agree,' he said, and suddenly she realized that his dark face, his white grin, his big, solid presence were not only comforting, they also promised safety. Protection.

'Would you mind — I know it is asking a lot — but would you mind terribly if I asked *you* to inform Geoff Holroyd who I am and what I've been doing here? I am planning to move just as soon as I can find a suitable place. I hate to admit it, Mr. Shipp, but I am always terrified he will be . . . ' she lowered her voice to a murmur ' . . . drunk, and that is so awkward and frightening for me.'

'I will be more than happy to do that, Miz Carruthers. By the way, there is a brand-new complex over on the other side of the river with big sunny apartments with glass walls. Should be just the thing for your work. I bet working here, with the draperies all closed, could give you claustrophobia.'

She nodded. 'Is there security at the new place?' she asked. 'I never realized before now just how important that can be.'

'They have a round-the-clock security guard who patrols the place on regular schedule. The complex is completely walled, with gardens, fishponds, flower-beds, and all kinds of amenities inside the enclosure. Nothing's completely secure, as you well know, but it's as near as you can get I think.' Shipp scribbled a number on a page from his notebook, tore it out and handed it to her.

'You call them and go take a look. If that doesn't suit you, somethin' else will. And good luck. We don't have so many celebrities in Templeton that we can have you moving off someplace else.'

When his wide back had passed through the front door, Cynthia breathed a sigh of relief. That had gone pretty well, and Mr. Shipp had been as nice as anyone could ask. Black or not, he was a gentleman.

Then she turned back to continue planning what she would sell to Ronald Henderson when he came. Afterward there would be the packing up. The thought of all that work made her feel suddenly faint.

She returned to the parlor and poured out another stiff shot of brandy. It might not be ladylike, but Papa and Mama had never been through anything like today, she felt sure, as the warmth of the liquor moved down her throat and eased her shivering.

She sat, warm and quiet in her deep chair, thinking of the new life she was about to create for herself.

Who would have supposed that a murder could be so beneficial? Or was that an irreverent thought?

'The hell with it,' said Cynthia Carruthers with a smile.

SUSAN OVEREDGE

So this was what it felt like to be faced with an impossible decision, Susan thought, as she watched Garth leave the Square for work. She had a dreadful feeling that he'd had something to do with the death of that man they found yesterday, and her dilemma lay in deciding whether or not she should risk doing something about it.

He had returned home from the office Sunday with some object inside his briefcase that made it almost twice as heavy as usual, when she put it away in the study. Was it a gun? The case was locked, of course, because Garth didn't trust her. He had always handled all the money, including the tiny inheritance she had from her mother — and he steadfastly refused to answer any questions about their finances.

If she pushed for replies he became angry and hit her. She had learned to creep about the house at night so well that she needed no light to find anything — including the key to Garth's desk. Even before the intruder had shown up, she systematically had gone through her husband's papers in the study with the door tightly closed and the drapes drawn shut. What she had found there sickened her. She always had entertained the hope that one day she would leave with the children and have her mother's little bit of money to tide them over until she found a teaching job.

But it was clear that not only had Garth's company been in trouble for a long time, he had spent all her money — along with his own — in an attempt to salvage things. She had taught accounting before their marriage, and the photocopies of invoices and communications from lawyers that he kept hidden away in the desk drawer told her all the things she hadn't wanted to know.

After this terrible discovery, Susan was ready to grab the kids and leave on the spot. She would ask her aunt to help until she found a job. But then this murder happened, bringing with it much larger issues than she felt she could handle.

She knew Garth left the house during Sunday night's storm. That fact was undeniable. When she'd asked where he was going, he gave her some excuse about getting a breath of air, even though it was pouring down with rain. She couldn't swear to it, but she thought she'd heard a gunshot close to the house, in between the constant loud cracks of thunder.

Shortly after her husband's departure, as Susan was still mulling over these events in her mind, Officer Shipp appeared on her front porch. She was almost relieved to see him. Even though she'd been raised to believe that it was a woman's duty to protect her husband, she had also been taught never to lie. If the truth got Garth into deep trouble, so be it. It wouldn't be her fault.

Wash was somewhat taken aback at her warm welcome. 'I have some questions to ask you, Miz Overedge,' he said. 'Then I'll talk to your husband at his office, once

I finish goin' 'round the Square. It's takin' more time than I expected.'

'I'm so glad you came,' she told him, leading the way into her sparse parlor, with its modern clean-lined furnishings and unencumbered by the usual Victorian bric-a-brac he had encountered in the previous houses on the Square. 'I do have something to tell you. It may help, and it may not — and it may make my husband appear in an unflattering light . . . '

'Just a moment,' Wash said. 'Before you say anything at all, let me tell you what *I* have learned from the victim's own record book. He was blackmailing several people around the Square. According to the notebook, the accuser claimed your husband was a wife and child abuser. He was threatening to expose Mr. Overedge to the authorities if he didn't pay up. So if you feel at all hesitant about speaking of such things, please be assured, we already are aware of that possibility.'

Susan felt her face go hot with a combination of shame and anger. So . . . *that* dreadful secret was no longer a secret. She sank in her chair, dizzy with relief.

Shipp, watching her closely, leaned forward. 'Now. Tell me what you wanted to say, Miz Overedge. Perhaps this makes it easier.'

'Yes, it does. And that . . . that last allegation is quite true. I have been trying to find a way to leave the area for months now. Garth has used all the money my mother left me to shore up his failing business, and . . . and planning my escape is taking some thought. What I wanted to tell you, though, is something else . . . '

Shipp nodded encouragingly, and she went on, 'Garth went in to his office Sunday afternoon. When he returned, his briefcase was much heavier than usual, and something inside shifted. I thought it felt as if it *might* be a pistol, although I didn't really think about that at the time.'

Shipp was making notes in his little black book as she spoke. 'About eight o'clock Sunday night, Garth went into his study and came out wearing his heavy raincoat. One pocket bulged, I couldn't swear to it — but it might have been a gun.

'He said he was going out to get some air, although it was pouring down with rain, and the lighting and thunder were striking constantly.' She paused, thinking back, reliving the tense moment while she waited for her husband to return from the garden behind the house.

'I couldn't see anything; the wind was whipping the shrubbery and the lightning blinded me, so I couldn't catch more than a glimpse outside. But even with all the booming thunder and lightning crackling, I think I heard a gunshot.'

She raised a protesting hand as Shipp began to say something. 'Now I can't swear to it, of course, because of the racket. But I was raised on a farm, Mr. Shipp. We shot all kinds of guns, from revolvers to twelve-gauge shotguns, and I know what a gunshot sounds like. There was one sound in all that noise that I believe might have been one.'

'That is as near as you can get?' Shipp asked.

'Yes. But I have to tell you that Garth

was inside again by eight-fifteen, and he had nothing with him that was long and hard like the stick or pipe they say struck the man and broke his neck. In other words, Mr. Shipp, I think Garth may have shot that man, but I'm pretty sure he didn't hit him as well. Garth doesn't hit people who are big enough to hit back.' She tried but could not control the bitterness in her voice.

Shipp nodded again. 'That would explain the wound in his arm, which, I should tell you, would not have been fatal. The position of the body was such that we judge he was coming from the *other* side of the Square when struck from behind. Quite possibly, if he had not been wounded the assailant might not have been able to overtake him.'

'So Garth *isn't* a murderer . . . quite,' she murmured.

'Probably not. But I thank you very much, Miz Overedge, for your courage in coming forward like this. Any information at all helps us. You understand that I must report the domestic abuse, particularly if it applies to the children. He did — does

— hit the children?'

'He beat Jessica several times — before I caught him at it. I threatened then to call Child Protective Services myself if he did it again, but I believe he did it anyway, while I was still pregnant with Chester. I'd find bruises on her from time to time that I couldn't account for.

'Then, when I found him shaking Chester as hard as he could — well, it was then that I realized I had to get the children out of here.'

'And what about you? Has he abused you?'

She paled. 'He *has* hit me, yes. Knocked me down, bloodied my nose. But I was raised to think everything was my own fault, and I'm just now beginning to realize that *he's* the one at fault. He is a hard, rough person, and he doesn't want to acknowledge that anyone else has feelings but him.'

'If he got counseling . . . ?' Shipp began, but she stopped him.

'No. I want to be able to live without being afraid every moment of the day. I want to earn my own living and take proper care of my children and be free of this . . . this mess. Can you understand that?'

'Oh, I can. And there may be a way I can help. How much money did he take from you? It may be . . . ' — but he didn't finish the thought.

To her surprise, Susan told him, 'Mother left me ten thousand dollars. I never saw a dime of it, because Garth took control of it from the beginning and kept it out of my reach. If I had that much right now, I could pay rent in a new place for a few months, get the children settled, and have time to find a really good job, instead of taking the first thing out there.'

Wash Shipp grinned at Susan, and his expression offered the first real hope for the future she had felt in a very long while. 'In East Texas there are ways to get things done. Not ways they'd condone in other places, maybe, but as long as they work to help people, what's the difference? Let me see what I can do.'

When he was gone, Susan plopped

into an uncomfortable steel and leather chair in the parlor and stared at the wall. Were she and her children about to be set free, after so many years of fear and servitude?

WASHINGTON SHIPP

Wash strolled back across the Park, thinking hard about this last bit of information from the Overedge household. He had eliminated Cynthia Carruthers as a suspect. Olivia Holt and her daughter were no longer even living in the Square. For various reasons, he had also eliminated Arthur Winchell and his daughter as likely candidates. And he was saving the Holroyds for last on his list. He still needed to question Milton Martin and Tom Allison and his family before tackling ol' Geoff Holroyd.

According to the notebook, Martin had paid, which could rule him out as the killer, Wash thought. If he'd intended to murder his blackmailer, surely he wouldn't have wasted five thousand dollars in cash beforehand? Still, he was the next on the list, so Wash made his way to Milton's door.

But the doorbell, somewhat to Wash's surprise, didn't work, so he began knocking briskly on the carved wooden door. Soon he heard the 'flap-flap' of the housekeeper Janey's slippers, and the lock clicked. One big brown eye peered around the door.

Once she recognized him, Janey threw open the door wide and ushered Wash into the front hall. 'Mr. Milton's in his room. I'll call him down. You go set in the parlor,' she commanded, and then she turned to climb the stairs.

Though he had spoken with Martin from time to time, usually while stopping at Carl's for coffee and a doughnut, Wash did not really know him intimately. Now, as the man entered the parlor, hair mussed, eyes bloodshot, face pale and unshaven, Wash was shocked at his appearance.

'I'm sorry, Mr. Martin. I didn't know you'd been ill,' he said. 'I could wait till another time, if you don't feel like talking right now.'

Martin shook his head. 'It's never going

to be a good time, Shipp. I have too much . . . too much stress going on right now, to be anything but sick.'

Wash now felt almost certain this disheveled fellow couldn't possibly have pulled off anything as stressful as killing someone. *Might as well clear this up right off*, he thought, accepting a cup of strong black coffee from Janey.

He set the delicate cup down and said, 'Mr. Martin, we need to get some things out in the open, so they needn't worry you so much. That fellow had a notebook in his possession that listed every family on the Square — and the things he knew about them.'

Martin turned even paler. 'You mean you know . . . ?'

'He knew about the . . . the terms of your discharge, yes. And I confirmed that fact when our computer whiz checked through your record. But unless you *killed* him, Mr. Martin, and I don't believe you did, this is irrelevant to the murder case. Unless something about all that changes, I know of no reason why those facts should ever be made public.'

Milton Martin, shaking visibly, buried his head into his hands. To his great consternation, Wash realized the other man was weeping.

'I c-couldn't kill anybody. Not even in the army. At W-west Point I faked it, but once I was in Korea it was too late to make things r-right. I r-ran away, Shipp. I left my m-men in the snow and caught a truck out of there. They all d-died.' He looked up and sniffed hard. 'As for k-killing a man with a stick, never in a million years could I do something like that.'

'You just sit tight, Mr. Martin.' Wash said. 'You just sit and wait for these things to be sorted out. This will probably never come to light, not unless some hotshot journalist digs it up, and that's not likely at all — now is it?' He reached over and patted the snuffling Martin on the shoulder.

Martin drew a shuddering breath and straightened up a bit. He lifted his own coffee cup and took a long sip.

'I paid the bastard,' he said finally, when he set the cup down. 'I sold some of my family heirlooms to do it. That's how much I wanted to keep this quiet. It . . . it's not the kind of thing a man wants to drag around behind him.'

Wash drained his own cup, set it aside, and stood. 'I suspect nobody need ever know 'bout this. We do things a bit different here than they're done in other places. That little notebook, for instance. Unless it has something to do with the murder itself, I suspect it won't turn out to be important evidence. I suspect it will 'get lost' somewhere. Chief Rawlinson agrees with me on that point — there's nobody needs the grief those notes could cause, if they got out.'

* * *

He left behind a much-relieved Martin, who climbed the stairs to shower, shave and comb his hair. Wash headed over toward the Allison house. This time he intended to interview Tom, asleep or not.

Sophia opened the door. She looked wary, but she greeted him politely and led him to the parlor. 'I'll get Tom, Mr.

Shipp. He's feeling much better, but he didn't go in to the office today. He knew you'd need to talk to him.'

While he waited, Wash looked about the room, noting the full bookshelves and the well-used desk. Metal filing cabinets against one wall were concealed by a stand filled with potted plants.

Tom Allison entered the room and held out an unsteady hand. Wash rose and shook it. The man *had* been sick, it was clear. A very bad cold would do that to you.

'I need to ask you just a few questions, Mr. Allison. But before I go into those, I must tell you what the victim had noted in his little book. This may help you understand just what I need to know from you.' Wash looked at his notes and read, 'Ernest. Helpless. Internet?

'I suspect this nasty piece of work intended to blackmail you or your son. He may have been planning it, but he might not have gotten to it yet. Can you tell me anything?'

Tom Allison sank into a chair, his eyes bright and his face flushed with fever. 'He *did* threaten my son with a computer message. He also sent me a note at work, wanting money to keep my son safe.'

He looked down at his hands, which were clenched in his lap. 'I don't pay extortion, Shipp. And I trained in a hard school, back in 'nam. I went out that night ready to kill him, but I can't tell you if I did or didn't.

'Somehow, everything got tangled up together . . . you ever hear of a flashback? I thought I was back in the jungle. I heard the man in the bushes, and I know I chased him, but whether I caught him or not, I can't tell you. My wife came out looking for me and found me in the front garden, draped over a rose bush and half out of my head. I must have been coming down with this fever before I went out, because I wouldn't have tripped or fallen like that in the jungle.

'I can tell you, that if I *had* caught up with him, I *would* have killed him, but I don't have any idea what actually happened.'

'What weapon did you have with you, that night?' Wash asked cautiously.

'Weapon?' Tom looked puzzled. 'I don't use or need weapons, Shipp. I used to do my killing with my hands and feet. If I had caught him, I would have killed him with my bare hands, probably with a chop to the side of the neck or a blow that ruptured a kidney.' He coughed deeply, his face flushing even redder.

Tom slumped sideways, and Wash jumped to catch him. The man was all but unconscious.

'Miz Allison! Call the doctor! I think your husband needs help — fast!' he yelled, as Sophia came rushing into the room.

She punched in 9-1-1 with shaking hands then knelt beside Tom, holding him steady. 'Will you help me get him upstairs? He's too heavy for me.'

Wash supported most of the man's weight, catching him under one arm, while Sophia took him under the other. Together they got him up the stairs and into the bedroom, where the rumpled covers spoke of troubled sleep and feverish tossing and turning.

'Did he say anything?' Sophia asked as

she pulled the covers smoothly over her husband's body. 'He went out, but I swear he didn't kill that man. He didn't have any weapons with him. *What did he tell you?*' She was beginning to sound as delirious as Tom.

Shipp led her out of the room. 'You'd better go down and let the doctor in,' he said. 'Now listen to me, your husband told me he went out that night. He also swore he took *no weapon*. But Saul Leeson was killed with a long heavy stick or a pipe.

'If those findings are accurate, Tom didn't use anything like that. His barehanded expeditions into the jungles of 'nam are still legendary in the military. I don't believe Tom Allison killed that man, though I suspect he would have, given half a chance. You just help him get well, and then maybe he'll remember what happened for himself.'

Sophia gave a sigh that was half a sob. Then she looked up at Wash, her chin firm, her jaw set. This was a woman who could handle things, he knew with sudden certainty.

'I attacked him myself,' she said finally.

'What?' Wash asked, stunned.

'Last week. I was sitting in the parlor, waiting to start supper, when someone came up on the porch out of the shrubbery at the side. He was in the door by the time I got to the hall. I snatched up a little statuette there and I hit him, hard, on the shoulder. He ran off . . .

'Then I went and got this pistol and I've kept it in my pocket ever since.' She patted her loose cotton shirt, which Wash realized sagged more than normal pocket contents would explain.

'A statuette?' he asked, recalling that tiny face-shaped bruise on the body's shoulder.

Sophia went down the stairs ahead of him and picked up an Oriental brass figure off a small table near the parlor door. Wash took it from her hand and hefted it. Heavy. And the face . . .

'Do you mind if I borrow this? We found a bruise, and I think this face would fit right into it,' he said.

'Feel free. It was a gift that I've hated since the day I opened the box. Lose it, if you can.' She managed a wavering smile. 'Or give it to somebody, if you have an enemy you want to torment.'

'I'll see what I can do,' Wash replied, wrapping the figure in a plastic bag and jamming it in his pocket.

* * *

As he moved toward the Holroyd house, he considered what he now knew: Two of the men in the Square had fully intended to kill Leeson, whether they had succeeded or not. What else was left to discover before this day was done?

As he passed his car parked in the Allison drive, the radio crackled and a message to return to the station came through loud and clear. Now what did the Chief want this morning? So far, he had taken little part in this business.

CHIEF RAWLINSON

Chief Rawlinson had hesitated to interrupt Wash with what he was doing, but he had a bad feeling about this affair. So, reluctantly, he had had the dispatcher call his assistant in before he could reach the Holroyd house.

Wash entered the office impatiently and took the single worn chair. 'Chief, I've got people with more motives than a dog has fleas,' he said. 'Everybody had some reason to kill Leeson, and most have owned up to it straight out. It might be Tom Allison, who can't say for sure whether he did it or not — I don't think so, though . . . '

He scratched his ear. 'That in itself is odd, you have to admit.' He pushed his notebook across the desk and Rawlinson leafed through it, reading rapidly.

When he looked up, he nodded. 'I

wondered about that,' he said, leaning back in his chair and reaching for the bottle holding his nitroglycerin tablets. He put one under his tongue then continued. 'That's why I wanted to talk to you before you tackle the Holroyds.'

'You know more about this bunch than I do,' Wash said. 'More than just the general gossip, I mean . . . '

'I went to school with Geoff,' the older man acknowledged. 'I knew his daddy well, and a worse-natured old bastard than Jesse, you never met. Arthur Winchell was a friend of Dad's. He almost married ol' Livvie Holt, though I think he thanked God every day of his life that her Mama didn't like the cut of his jib and put a stop to it.'

Rawlinson closed his eyes. 'I think it may help you to understand these folks if I give you some input. The Holts seem to be well out of it now, and the Overedges are relative newcomers, but the rest of 'em I know well.

'Milton Martin was bullied by his Daddy every day of his life. He was no more suited to the military than a lapdog, but he was a good student and he passed all the academics with flying colors. I figured he'd be in trouble if we got into a war, though he'd have been a good officer in a peacetime army. Evidently I was right.

'But I swear to you that that boy could no more kill somebody than he could buck his Daddy.'

'I'd already come to that conclusion,' Wash agreed. 'He seems like a nice enough fellow, but not a man of action, whatever else he may be.'

'Tom Allison's grandpa took up the lease on Number Six after the old Mitchells died of flu in 1918,' the Chief went on. 'I knew his folks fairly well, though Tom was too much younger for me to have much truck with. When you're young, a few years can seem like a lot.'

'You liked him, though?' Wash asked. 'Did you have much to do with him after he came home from Vietnam?'

'Not much, though I remember him as being a pretty solid youngster. He had set his mind on marrying Sophia before he was drafted, and when he came back, he was still of the same mind. She was mightily upset about his drug and alcohol abuse, but I suspect she thought she could cure him with love.'

He sighed deeply. 'Didn't quite work that way, of course. Somebody as messed up as Tom was needed professional help, and I tried to find a way for him to get it without Sophia knowing. That took a long time — years, in fact.

'In the meanwhile Ernest was born, and Sophia just about went crazy herself when she realized her boy was so handicapped. Blamed Tom, blamed his drug use, though that probably had nothing to do with it. But that's not much comfort.

'Even when Tom began straightening out, and making a go of his law practice, she still held Ernest's handicaps against him, I think.'

Wash smiled then. 'You know, I think all this upset has been sort of a shock treatment for that marriage. Sophia's ready to do battle for her menfolk now. That's one determined little lady — she admitted she was the one who hit Leeson and left that odd bruise on him. But I don't believe either one of them had anything to do with the murder itself.'

Rawlinson nodded. 'And you really don't need to worry any more about Cynthia Carruthers. I see by your notebook that you found out her guilty little secret, which might *bother* her some, but certainly wouldn't be much of a motive for murder. Besides, she's a might too wispy to get in a good lick, I'd think.

'You know the Winchells as well as I do, of course. 'Nuf said there . . . So it's mainly Geoff and his sister left. It isn't just the fact that they've got fingers in all the richest pies around town. They're odd people, and I wanted you to know what I know before you go talk to them.'

He shuffled the stack of papers before him and brought out a sheet on which he'd written his notes. Damn memory wasn't worth a hang any more, but he'd put down everything that might be of help to his assistant.

'Geoff was always a skirt-chaser and a drunk, just like his Daddy, though he didn't have the backbone old Jesse had. He got three girls in our class pregnant before we were seniors, and back then that was a mighty big deal. If their folks hadn't known what a rotter he was, he'd have had a shotgun wedding for sure, but even then an illegitimate grandchild was better than having Geoff Holroyd for a son-in-law.

'When he went to Korea, I was already in the army in Germany, so I didn't know much about what happened there. He came back a few months after I was discharged, and you'd a' thought he'd tackled the Chinese army single-handed, to hear him talk. Of course, I didn't believe any of it — just a bunch of hot air.

'Then he learned to fly and got into that so-called 'Confederate Air Force.' You know, that group that put on flying exhibitions all over the country at air shows. I knew he drank too much to be flying, but old Doc Jennings was such a friend of the Holroyds that he certified him as fit.

'Then Geoff had that god-awful accident. Jennings had to cover his own tail and swear Geoff wasn't drunk at the time. I knew better, and a lot of the others did too, but you know how hard it is to confuse people with facts when they'd rather believe a lie.'

He looked down at the sheet in his hands. 'Geoff is a bad one, Wash, and he's weak. But Marilyn isn't.'

Wash sat up straight. 'Miz Marilyn? She'd be how old now? In her early sixties?'

'Marilyn Holroyd is a proper, rather stern woman who looks like she wouldn't hurt a fly.' Rawlinson struggled for a moment with his sense of propriety before continuing, 'But I always suspected she had a hand in her Daddy's death.'

'Ol' Mr. Jesse? But he'd been sick for years when he died.' Wash looked at his mentor in bewilderment.

'I know . . . I know, Wash. And I felt like he should have been shot years before he went. Still, I wasn't quite satisfied with things when I went — I was just an ordinary cop then — to help take Jesse out of the house. I managed to corner the coroner, and convince him to take a blood sample before the mortuary got hold of the body.'

Wash's eyes opened wide. 'And what did the blood test show?'

Rawlinson crumpled the paper between both hands. 'Well, that's just it. Dr. Jennings found out about the blood sample. He got hold of it and it's not been seen since. But I have wondered for years if Marilyn might have helped her Daddy along. And it looks as if Saul Leeson had been wondering the same thing.'

He pointed to the cryptic line copied from Leeson's notebook. 'All the rest of these folks have been pretty open with you, Wash. By the way, I take it you haven't talked to the Overedges yet . . . ' He paused, because Wash was grinning at him.

'What are you up to?'

'I might just get in a spot of blackmail myself, when I have my talk with Garth Overedge,' Wash said. 'I did talk to Susan Overedge, and she confirmed Leeson's charges of Garth's physical abuse to his family. Also she accused Garth of taking the bit of money she inherited from her mother without asking her. She wants to get away from here and . . .'

' . . . And you're going to trade him your silence on the abuse charges for his giving back her money. I like it, Wash. I like it a lot. Some folks might consider it unethical, but here it's just the way we do business. Overedge stole from his wife and abused her too. Now he's going to pay through the nose, eh? And we're just the guys to see to it.' Rawlinson began to laugh out loud.

Wash joined in. 'I thought you'd like that. Not often do we get such a chance to see justice is done. God knows the courts seldom follow through and see to it.

'When I finish interviewing the Holroyds, I intend to pin down Overedge in his office and 'urge' him to do the right thing. That poor woman and her kids need to get away from him. She's a schoolteacher, so she shouldn't have too much trouble finding work.'

Trust old Wash to figure out a way to make something useful come out of this mess. Not often, nowadays, did the Chief have cause to feel quite that good about anything.

'Now about the Holroyds,' he said. 'You watch their faces, when you talk to them. Listen to the tone of their voices. I doubt their words are going to tell you much, but I have a gut feeling they know a lot more than they've let on. If nothing else, their house commands a great view of that whole area where the body was found.'

He felt a warning twinge and put another tablet under his tongue. 'Won't be long Wash, before you'll be taking over for me. Six months until my retirement — not a minute too soon for me.

'You be careful of these folks,' he warned. 'They've got a lot of pull, and if you make enemies of them, they'll make it rough on you.' He began to wheeze, and Wash rose to leave.

'Take care of yourself, Chief,' he said. 'And I'll take care of everything else. I've learned the hard way how to get things done around here, without lettin' on what I'm doin'.'

Watching his assistant's broad back move resolutely down the hall, Rawlinson reflected on that statement. It was true, and he felt a bit guilty about it, even though he'd always done his best to see that everybody, whatever the color, was treated right in Templeton, Texas. In his thirty years in office, that had not always been easy, and it had been people like the Holroyds, in many cases, who made it harder than it should have been.

GEOFFREY HOLROYD

Yesterday had been one hell of a day. Today looked as if it might become even worse, Geoff thought. He poured himself another drink, but somehow his usual solace wasn't working this afternoon.

All morning he had watched Washington Shipp go around the Square, talking with the Holroyd tenants. The Allison house was the last, except for his and the Winchell place, and somehow Geoff thought Shipp would handle old Arthur, his mentor, with kid gloves. Now, it was his turn to be interviewed.

He was surprised then, when Shipp climbed in his car after leaving the Allisons and drove out of the Square. What happened, he wondered, to interrupt the man's methodical route? The respite gave him a little more time to drink, he thought, until he realized that he should have his wits about him while being interrogated. He might be tempted to let slip things that should be kept secret.

When the buzzer informed him Shipp's car was returning, Geoff poured himself one last Scotch. It was time to step up like a man. He tossed off the drink, straightened his clothing, and checked his appearance in a mirror so old and silvered it seemed to hold ghostly shadows of the many reflections it had known.

He moved out onto the veranda as Shipp was letting himself in the front gate. He looked up and nodded, and Geoff gestured for him to seat himself in one of the wicker porch chairs. 'Nice and cool out here now,' he said. 'Seems as if there's a breath of fall, this afternoon.'

Shipp sat down carefully, testing the old chair's strength before risking his considerable bulk to it. Reassured, he settled back and pulled his ever-present notebook from his pocket.

'You've probably seen me goin' up and down the Square earlier today, talkin' to all the people here,' the officer began.

'Since the victim was a relative of yours, I saved you for last, thinking you might know something more about him that would aid in our investigation.'

Geoff snorted. 'I knew Saul when he was a kid, of course — bratty little snot he was, too. Always stickin' his nose in where he wasn't wanted. I was an adult when he first came to visit our folks, and so was Marilyn. Father was — let me see — I guess Dad was Saul's *great*-uncle, though I don't keep close tabs on that family tree sort of thing. Dog kin, they used to call it, and he was just the pup to prove it.'

'So he was curious 'bout stuff even then?' Wash asked. 'Pokin' into local gossip 'n' things? Did he get into stuff in *your* family's house, do you know? He kept a list of items he evidently has stolen, including from your place, in the past few weeks.'

'Stolen? From us? Well, Marilyn will be furious, I can tell you! She loves that old stuff. I guess it's a remembrance of our family to her. I'm afraid, I never paid much attention to what little Saul was up to. I was in and out, mostly. Had my own fish to fry, you know.'

Shipp turned a few pages in his notebook, re-checking some of the information he had gleaned from others on the Square. 'Sunday night was stormy here, wasn't it? Thunder and lightnin' — so it's not likely anybody can remember hearin' the shot.'

'Shot?' Geoff mulled over what he had overheard about the murder. If Marilyn had mentioned a gunshot wound, he had been too woozy to catch it. 'You mean he was shot to death instead of having his neck broke?'

Shipp shook his head. 'Both,' he replied, with admirable brevity. 'Shot first, not fatally, then he was hit across the back of the neck with something round and heavy, about three-quarters of an inch in diameter. Must have been fairly long, too, because of the force of the blow. Thing shattered his top three vertebrae and severed his spinal cord. *Somebody* took a powerful swing with it.'

Geoff shuddered. He hadn't *liked* the sonofabitch, but he wouldn't wish that kind of damage on anybody.

Shipp was watching him carefully. 'What was the reaction, locally I mean, when he married Arthur Winchell's daughter — do you recall?'

'You mean in *our* family, or amongst the neighbors?' Geoff asked, thinking back.

'Both.'

'Well, we in the family thought the young lady was making a huge mistake. We all figured Saul for a stinker from the word go. On the other hand, most of the neighbors seemed to think it was her last chance to make a good match, poor girl, and she'd better grab him before he changed his mind.

'Lots of those old biddies — most of 'em are dead now — were a gossipy bunch. I know for certain they counted the months down while Maggie's first baby was on the way. You never saw such disappointment when Saul and Maggie moved out to California and they had to depend on word of mouth instead of observation.'

'I've seen it happen that way, too,' Shipp said. 'Makes you kind of sick, doesn't it?'

'Damn right. It was none of their business . . . ' Geoff paused and regrouped. He was too groggy by far to risk letting this man make him relax and spill something that would make him suspicious.

'Did you know Saul Leeson knew the truth about your flying accident?' Shipp asked suddenly. 'He had a notebook on him when he died, and in it there were remarks about just about everyone here in the Square. He thought . . . '

'I can imagine what he thought!' Geoff erupted, feeling his face flush hot and red. 'Figured I was drunk, did he? Thought I crashed that plane through negligence — and killed all those people . . . ' — again he stopped short, fearing he was going too far.

'Well . . . ' he mumbled, sinking back in his chair and reaching blindly for a glass, though there was not one on the rattan table beside him. 'At least no charges were ever filed . . . '

'Oh, we know that,' Shipp reassured him. 'We just wanted to know if he ever contacted you, trying to make you think he might have proof of something. Did he ever ask you for money to keep quiet?'

'Never!' *That* was one thing Geoff knew he would have remembered, no matter how drunk he might have been at the time.

'Then that's all I needed to discuss with you, Colonel,' Shipp said. He rose and looked toward the front door. 'Now, I'll need to speak with Miz Marilyn, please. May I go and call her?'

'You go right ahead,' Geoff told him. As Wash disappeared into the wide doorway, Geoff shivered, as if someone — or some-*thing* — had walked over his grave. There *had* been something, that Sunday evening, besides seeing the furtive shape slinking through the shrubbery. Something he couldn't quite recall, though it made him uneasy when he fished through his unready memory after it.

For some reason he kept thinking about Marilyn's damn potted plants, but the thought escaped him. When he heard Marilyn's voice in the front hall, Geoff slipped around to the side door and headed for his study and the bottle. He'd done his duty. Now it was time to get stinking.

MARILYN HOLROYD

She had known this day would come, and the thought had terrified her. Never had Marilyn come so close to disaster, and the thought of being interrogated was appalling. Nevertheless, she welcomed Wash Shipp warmly into the parlor.

As they took their seats, she heard a faint crinkle of paper and froze. Had *he* heard that too? But evidently the note pinned securely inside her bra had not betrayed her.

Clasping her hands tightly in her lap, she forced a smile, as Wash opened his notebook. Lawmen used those little notebooks as weapons, she thought suddenly. You couldn't help but wonder what others had said before that might contradict what you intended to say now.

But surely nobody had seen that vague shape in the rain pause in the side portico and slip his filthy note under the screen door. *Had they?* It was only by luck that she retrieved it before Lutetia discovered it. Not that Lutetia would ever betray her employers, but it was best that such things be kept secret.

'I take it you didn't go outside Sunday evening, Miz Holroyd?' Shipp looked down at the notebook again, and she was afraid to lie.

'I *did* go out onto the side portico. I wanted to see how far up the flood had come. It must have been something like seven-thirty or maybe even eight o'clock when I stepped out. But the rain was blowing in under the shelter so hard that I came right back in.' She closed her eyes in concentration then continued.

'Actually, I thought I saw someone near the wall between us and the Carruthers place, but it was just a quick impression . . . probably a bush blowing in the wind. The light was bad, alternating between flashes of lightning and pitch darkness, and the leaves were shining, wet with rain . . . ' There. She hoped that would cover anything anyone else might have reported earlier.

'Oh yes. Geoff mentioned he thought he saw somebody out there a little earlier, so I might have been influenced by that.' This, too, was entirely true.

Shipp nodded, his expression thoughtful. 'The doctor who examined Leeson's body says he was killed with a rod or pipe about three-quarters of an inch in diameter and perhaps as much as four feet long. Have you seen anything like that here or elsewhere among your neighbors? It might be a pole used to hold up shrubbery or a pipe used for reinforcing something. Anything at all.'

Marilyn felt herself go pale. 'My plant holder rod on the veranda is about that length and size. It lies between the wrought-iron hooks fastened to the posts on the east end of the porch, and I hang my pots of fern on it. But it's right where it ought to be.'

'Let's go look at it, shall we?' He rose and waited for her to precede him to the veranda.

She moved quickly, hearing his step just behind her. She drew a sigh of relief when she found the rod in place, showing no evidence that it had been moved.

'See? It's there, and there's no sign . . .' — she peered closely at the thick masses of Boston fern — ' . . . no sign that the plants have been disturbed.'

But there was, and she had just realized it. They were on opposite ends of the rod. The trailing one had been at the left, the cropped one at the right. She must show no sign of anything, she knew, so she managed to look calm.

'Good,' Wash said. 'Much of what we do is eliminate the possibilities. However, would you mind a great deal if we took that rod and had it checked out? It has to go to Dallas, and the sooner it goes on its way the better.'

'I . . . I feel so weak. Would you mind lifting it down? I'm not used to this sort of . . . of thing,' she said, dropping into the chair nearest the end of the porch.

Shipp carefully lifted the rod from the brackets, keeping the swinging pots level, and lowered it to the floor. 'Will the ferns be all right sitting there?' he asked.

'Probably. Sometimes the cats get into

them, but they should do all right here until you get the rod back to me.' She felt her heart begin to gallop, making the paper crinkle, so faintly she could barely hear it herself.

Wash took a sheet of pliofilm from his pocket and wrapped it around the rod, tying off the loose ends. 'Thank you, Miz Holroyd. It shouldn't take more than a week or ten days to get it checked. They are pretty well swamped up there, or it would be sooner.'

He looked around for Geoff, but Marilyn made a helpless gesture toward the study. 'He's probably in there . . . drinking.'

Shipp nodded understandingly and turned away. She watched him move down the street to his car. Then Marilyn drew a shuddering breath and hurried into the house, climbing at once to her room.

There she took off her blouse and unpinned the note. 'Yu kild yor daddy,' it said in straggling letters. 'I no it and I kin prove it. If yu don't want to go to jale, put $5000 in the lektrik box at the dock on Sundy nite.'

She could hardly believe that her cousin

Saul, who had been a child she had known, could do such a thing. How *could* he know? Papa had been sick the last time he came, but Saul had been gone for years and was almost grown by the time she gave that overdose of painkiller.

Even if she had been willing to pay for silence, she could not have gone to the dock on Sunday night, for the flood had already moved past the post holding the circuit box before she got the note. No, she had understood that drastic action was called for.

She knew little about the law, but she did understand there was no statute of limitations on murder. And now she had done it twice. She could still feel the cold smoothness of the rod in her hands as she waited for that slinking figure to appear in the storm. It had been pure luck that she caught a glimpse of him as he emerged from the Allison yard and ran up through the Park, as though making for her own home.

She'd sped through the trees, and his steps had come intermittently to her ears as he followed the winding path. At the point where she waited, it turned back toward the west, and she had hit him as hard as she could when she saw him. The crunch of shattering bone had haunted her since that night.

Now Marilyn knew Washington Shipp would find the truth. There was a look in his eye, in the set of his shoulders, and in the determination of his chin to assure her of that. No matter how well she had cleaned the rod, they would probably find traces of blood or hair, when they sent it to Dallas.

She went heavily down the stairs and looked into the study. 'I'm not feeling well,' she said to her brother. Lutetia, passing on her way to the kitchen, looked up, concerned.

'I think I've caught cold. I'm going to take some medicine and go to bed. Wake me in the morning, but don't bother me before then. I'll try to sleep it off.' She turned and went upstairs again.

She had not disposed of all of Papa's painkiller after he died. There should be just about enough. She had no intention of going through an arrest and a trial and, quite probably, an execution.

ARTHUR MELLINGHAM WINCHELL

I'm too old for this, Arthur thought. He was sitting in the rattan chair on his veranda, keeping an eye on young Sammy while Margaret finished preparing dinner. The other children were in the back garden, playing on the swings and yelling as if they were being tortured by fiends.

The Square seemed quiet now, the gates locked again against any intrusion from the street. Yet the peace of the place had been disrupted, and nobody here, he suspected, felt the security they had all known before Monday morning.

To his surprise, Margaret had gone down to the police station and made a full statement. When she returned, she looked more relaxed than she had in a very long time, but she wouldn't answer his questions. He could only surmise that she had made a clean breast of her payments to Saul, while she pretended he was dead and kept collecting his insurance and his pension.

Now the bastard was actually dead, Arthur wondered what complications would arise from that. Perhaps they would only withhold payments until they had recovered what was paid while Saul still lived. Then, perhaps, they could be made to begin paying again. A woman with children had to have an income, and he still had some strings he could pull.

'I may be in my nineties,' he told Sammy, who was pushing a toy truck up and down the length of one of the planks in the flooring. 'I may be old and doddery, but I can still get things done, if I need to.'

Sammy looked up. He hadn't said anything more about his father's death, but Arthur felt sure he would, sooner or later. What the boy said was not what he expected to hear.

'You know, Grampa, I'm glad somebody killed Daddy. He worried Mama most to death. I used to sneak downstairs when he came home and listen to them. Daddy was a mean man, wasn't he, Grampa?'

Arthur hated to admit it to the man's own son, but he had to. 'Yes, Sammy, he was. I expect your mother will settle down and relax a bit, now she knows for sure he won't come back to bother her.'

Sammy zoomed his truck all the way to the end of the porch and back before speaking again. 'Things sure have changed,' he said, sitting beside Arthur's chair to rest. 'I heard Miz Overedge talking to Effie.'

'Miz Holt's maid? What did she say?' Arthur asked.

Sammy squinched his eyes, thinking hard. 'Effie said Miz Elma was putting her mama in a home and is going to live with her husband. They won't need Effie, and the lease is going back to Mr. Holroyd.'

Arthur shifted his weight from one bony buttock to the other and sighed. Things that had seemed unchangeable were suddenly changing fast. Enough to unsettle anybody, particularly someone as old as he.

'Hear any more gossip?' he asked his grandson.

Sammy nodded. That boy got around as quietly as an Indian and seemed to hear all kinds of unexpected things. Now he came up with another tidbit.

'Miz Overedge told Effie *she* was going to move, too. She's taking Jessica and Chester to her aunt's to live. I guess Mr. Overedge'll have to live all by himself.'

Arthur smiled. *Fat chance!* he thought. Garth Overedge living without someone to serve as slave and whipping boy was hard to imagine. 'I expect that house will be empty too,' he observed.

That would make three. Cynthia Carruthers already had told Margaret that she was moving away. It was as if a tornado had swept through the quiet confines of the Square, picking up families at random and casting them out into the wide world.

'An' I saw old Janey in the Park this morning, too,' Sammy told him.

'I thought your Mama told you to stay out of the Park until everythin' settles down,' Arthur said, his tone sharp.

'But all that was Monday. This is today, and there's nothin' there now but some yellow tape,' the boy objected. 'Besides, Janey was sittin' on a bench, and I visited with her for a while. She said Mr. Martin's going to move back to Atlanta. He's selling off all the stuff in his house and will be going as soon as that's done. I wish he'd give me that little jade dolphin he showed me once; I think it's neat.'

'So what about the Allisons?' Arthur asked. 'You're better than the TV, Sam. I can get all the news I want without ever moving off the porch.'

Sammy looked thoughtful. 'Miz Allison smiles more now,' he said finally. 'She used to look like she'd been eatin' sour pickles. Mr. Allison's been sick, but the doctor says he don't have to go to the hospital or nothin'.

'Then, when I was just passin' by . . . ' — he looked sideways at his grandfather, and Arthur knew he was sidestepping the forbidden word 'eavesdropping' — ' . . . I heard Ernest answering the phone. He never used to be downstairs, ever — and he never used to answer the phone.

'He told somebody he was gonna go to *thurippy* — what's that, Grampa? And he said his folks were going to move to Dallas to be close to him.'

'Therapy means that trained people are going to teach Ernest how to deal with his problems. He's been kept so close over there that it's a wonder he's even sane. As it is, he may be the sanest person on the Square.'

Given the situation, that wasn't too far from the truth, Arthur realized. 'Of all the places I've ever been,' he mused aloud, 'This is the last I'd ever have thought would produce a murder. I've stood on battlefields with people dying all around me. I've watched my wife die by inches. But I never thought I'd see something like this, right here in Holroyd Square.'

Margaret stepped out onto the porch and said, 'Come in to dinner, now. Sammy, have you washed? Your brothers are just about through in the downstairs bathroom.' Her voice was softer, gentler, less strained than it had been for years.

With a deep groan, Arthur rose and

pulled Sammy to his feet. 'Let's go, Sam Hill,' he said.

As they went into the house, he found himself hopeful once more. Maybe things would be better now. He felt suddenly as if ninety-four might not be the end of the road after all. He had to keep an eye on Sammy. That boy was going to make his mark in the world, or Arthur was badly mistaken.

WASHINGTON SHIPP

Wash felt good. He stood, all soaped up, in the shower, singing 'Old Man River' and making the walls vibrate with his bass tones. He'd learned a lot yesterday, and maybe today he would be able to put together all the pieces of the puzzle he had listed in his notebook. He felt he might be right on the edge of solving this crime.

The shower curtain rustled as Jewel's voice interrupted his thoughts. 'Phone, Wash. The station. You'd better dry off and come right now.'

Shipp groaned and reached for the towel she was handing him. He donned his robe and rubbed at his hair with the towel as he flapped in his shower clogs toward the telephone in the hall.

''Lo,' he said.

'Sir, sorry to disturb you so early, but

there has been a 911 call from Lutetia Masters in Holroyd Square. She wouldn't say what the problem was, but she did insist that you needed to get over there in person. She said it is an emergency. Can you go now?'

'Yes, I'm on it,' he said. 'I'll be there in ten minutes.'

Jewel had his clothing ready, his keys laid out, and all he had to do was dress and go. *What on earth,* he wondered, could have caused Lutetia to call for him so early?

He paused and honked at the gates and was quickly buzzed in. He drove in and stopped in the Holroyd drive, where Lutetia was waiting for him under the portico at the side.

'Wash, you better come with me right now. We got a big problem here.' Without further explanation, she turned into the side door and hurried him through the kitchen, into the hall, and up the stairs.

'You go on in. I can't seem to make myself go back,' the woman said, her voice tight with pain.

Wash opened the old paneled door and

looked into a large bedroom lit by three wide windows. The bed was on his left, and on it was a shape lying entirely too still, even for a sound sleeper.

Oh, God! he thought, turning back to Lutetia. 'Marilyn Holroyd?' he asked. She nodded.

He moved nearer and saw the neat gray braid, the cyanotic face, the hand lying on the sheet, clenching a bit of paper. He ached to know what was written there, but he knew he would have to wait until the judge had done his thing and pictures had been taken.

'Why did she do it, Lutetia — and how?' he asked the old servant. 'Do you have any idea at all?'

Lutetia sank onto a small chair in the hall and covered her face with both hands. 'I 'spect she saved some of Mr. Jesse's medicine. I never found the rest after he died. I always wondered if she'd . . . she'd helped him along, you know? He was a heller, even if he was my daddy . . . ' She lowered her hands and stared defiantly at Wash.

'And Miz Mar'lyn was my half-sister.

Lord, Wash, what we goin' to do?'

He turned out of the room and lifted her to her feet to give her a reassuring hug. 'You go on down and tell Mr. Geoff, as best you can. I'll call this in and get things started. I 'spect this is goin' to solve that other murder, Lutetia, don't you?'

''Fraid so, Wash. 'Fraid so,' she said, as she turned to descend the stairs.

* * *

The note, when all the formalities were taken care of, was very simple:

> I killed my father, and I killed the man who left the note I have placed on my dresser, though I didn't know it was Saul at the time. I just hit him as hard as I could with the planter pole.
>
> I can't face what comes next. Geoff, I'm sorry, but you'll have all the money now and can drink yourself to death. Lutetia, you've been more a sister than Geoff was ever a brother. I'm leaving you enough to be

comfortable without working.

Maybe God will be merciful after I'm dead. He never was while I was alive.

Marilyn Holroyd

Poor woman, Wash thought as he sat with the Chief and Judge Ennis at the quiet hearing that closed both cases. No reporters were present. Nothing would be published that would sully the Holroyd name.

Geoff, sitting up front, looked stunned. Maybe this would be the shock the man needed, Wash thought. If nothing else, living on the Square alone with only the Winchells left paying him lease money, might make him pull up his socks.

Then Wash thought of the six lively Winchell grandsons. The Square might be mostly empty of tenants, but the noise level couldn't do anything but grow, he was certain.

Arthur, sitting just behind him, leaned forward and touched his shoulder. 'It's best,' he muttered softly. 'Get this out of the way, and things are bound to get better. Those are good houses. Send us some respectable prospects, Wash. Any color, you hear? I'll help Geoff choose good ones, if I can.

'Maybe, when things settle down, the Square will be a nice place to live again.'

Wash rose with the rest and made his way out of the courthouse. Chief Rawlinson turned to him and held out his hand. 'I got word from the commission this morning,' he said. 'I just got early retirement on account of my heart. You're in charge now, Wash. You take care of my people, you hear?'

Jewel was coming to meet them, beaming. She had already heard the news then. It didn't surprise him — she was usually about ten yards ahead of everybody else, and it was clear she had heard.

* * *

He went to join her, and they strolled together out into the bright September day. He wondered, as he felt her hand close about his, if he would ever have another case as strange as this one. Still, being in East Texas, he figured the next one would probably be even stranger.

THE END

Other titles in the
Linford Mystery Library:

SHERLOCK HOLMES TAKES A HAND

Vernon Mealor

An exciting trio of tales following the escapades of Colonel Sebastian Moran, 'one of the best shots in the world' and the 'second most dangerous man in London', according to Sherlock Holmes. Find out how Moran achieves his position at the right hand of Professor Moriarty in 'The Hurlstone Selection'; shares lodgings with Holmes, Watson, and Mrs Hudson in 'The Man with the Square-Toed Boots'; and turns his skills to art theft in 'The Disappearance of Lord Lexingham'.

THE THIRD KEY

Gerald Verner

The Reverend Colin Armitage receives a parcel one morning containing a key and the intriguing message: 'This is Bluebeard's first key.' The key belongs to the cottage of a woman named Sylvia Shand, who is found there, strangled. A few days later, Bluebeard's second key arrives by post and the district nurse is found strangled in similar circumstances. The police believe a homicidal maniac is loose in the village but Armitage has other ideas. And then a third key arrives . . .

MORE CASES OF A PRIVATE EYE

Ernest Dudley

This second book of Ernest Dudley's stories about his London-based private eye character, Nat Craig, finds Craig's clients making up a pretty varied collection. Young, wealthy women getting themselves blackmailed; wealthier men or women who have the jitters over the safety of their precious family heirlooms; occasionally even members of the ex-crook class, appeal to him for help. And not infrequently Craig finds himself confronted with grisly murders, testing his tough resourcefulness and considerable powers of deduction.

Classic British crime stories with an intriguing psychological slant on characters from every walk of life!

A CANDIDATE FOR CONSPIRACY

Steve Hayes

Yesterday he was a spy. Today he's a Washington politician. Tomorrow he could be the next President of the United States. Soon he could be in control of one of the world's most powerful nations — unless a daredevil adventurer and his beautiful accomplice can stop him. But that's a big if . . .

THE ROYAL FLUSH MURDERS

Gerald Verner

Superintendent Budd is called in by the local police of Long Millford to investigate the strange murder of John Brockwell, impaled to the trunk of a tree with a pitchfork. Pinned to the lapel of the dead man's jacket is a playing card: the ten of diamonds. What is the meaning of this sign left on the body? Who hates the unpleasant Brockwell family so intensely, and why?